WILD KILLER

TYSON WILD BOOK SEVEN

TRIPP ELLIS

WELCOME

Want more books like this?

You'll probably never hear about my new releases unless you join my newsletter.

SIGN UP HERE

1

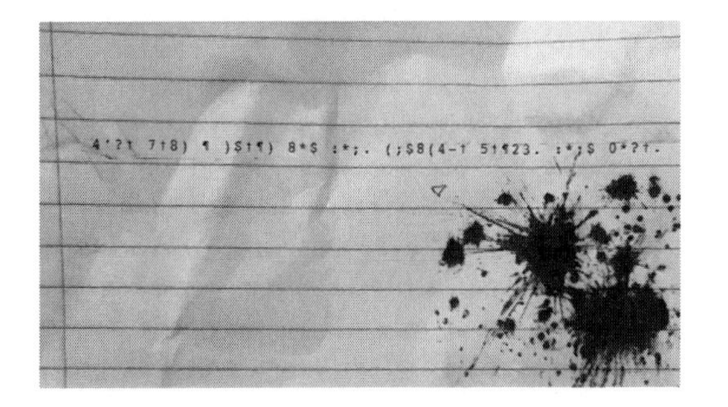

It was another gruesome reminder. The bloodstained, coded message that Reagan had received was a clear indication that the *Sandcastle Killer* was still active and didn't have any plans on retiring soon.

I had every intention of forcing him into retirement.

So far, we had nothing to go on.

And the bodies were beginning to pile up.

Reagan MacKenzie had become the killer's press contact—his conduit to the outside world. The local reporter, known for her consumer advocacy, had been thrust into the limelight and had quickly established herself as a voice of authority regarding all things related to the *Sandcastle* murders.

Of course, receiving direct communication from a sadistic killer was a bit unsettling. Reagan was currently occupying the guest suite aboard the *Wild Tide.* The killer knew where she lived, and Reagan didn't feel comfortable staying home alone, which meant I had an indefinite houseguest. Not that I minded too terribly much. She was easy on the eyes.

Very easy.

Reagan had a sharp tongue, and a sassy personality, which wasn't a bad thing, but she could be a bit of a handful from time to time.

I was never one to back down from a challenge.

My stomach twisted in anticipation of the horrors I would find at the latest dumpsite. It had only taken a few hours for the lab to decode the cryptic message. Though, Elijah—one of the tech gurus at the TV station—had decoded it in less time.

The message read: *I've left a treat for you. Surfside Beach. Your move.*

It was a sick, sadistic game—one the killer thoroughly enjoyed.

The wind whistled through my helmet as I twisted the throttle. I raced through Coconut Key atop my *Yamazuki X6* sport-bike—600 cc of pure adrenaline. The exhaust howled, and the crotch rocket devoured the pavement. The scenery blurred by. The motorcycle was an angel and a devil, all wrapped into a sleek, aerodynamic package. It could dispense copious amounts of pleasure and pain. One wrong move, one blip of the throttle, one miscalculation and the sublime ballet of rider and machine could turn into a devastating demolition derby. I tried to keep the damn thing to a reasonable speed, but it was easy to get into the triple digits without too much effort.

JD's red Porsche was in the parking lot when I pulled in. Sheriff Daniels, the medical examiner, and the forensics team were already scouring the beach by the time I arrived.

Reagan showed up with a news crew before I had killed the engine. The door to the van slid open, and she hopped out along with a cameraman.

I pulled off my helmet, and in a flash, Reagan had shoved a microphone in my face. The cameraman lensed me up.

"Have you discovered another body?" Reagan asked with the camera rolling.

She knew I didn't know anymore than she did at this point.

"I just got here."

"Have you been able to establish the authenticity of the latest note from the killer?"

"The crime lab tells me it's authentic."

I climbed off the bike and strolled toward the beach.

Reagan and her crew followed.

She scowled at me when I told her the beach was closed and the crew would have to remain in the parking lot. "Sorry, this is an active crime scene."

Her eyes soured, and I knew she would give me an earful later.

I trudged through the sand toward the congregation of county employees. JD greeted me wearing his standard uniform—Hawaiian shirt, cargo shorts, and sport sandals. He usually wore those, or a pair of checkered *Vans*. His long hair flowed in the breeze, and his mirrored aviator sunglasses reflected the teal blue ocean. Seagulls squawked overhead, and the surf crashed against the white sand. It would have been a nice morning if it weren't for the fact we were looking for a dead body.

JD shook his head. "I think we're getting the runaround."

"What do you mean?" I asked.

"No body."

The *Sandcastle Killer* had a habit of burying bodies underneath the sand. His nickname stemmed from the fact that a little boy, attempting to build a sandcastle, found the first body. The name stuck. There were also several other disconcerting patterns of behavior the *Sandcastle Killer* exhibited. Up to this point, every victim had been found in a similar condition.

My eyes scanned the beach. Sheriff Daniels and the others were scattered about, searching for the remains, poking at the sand. I had a pretty good idea of who they were looking for.

"Maybe he dumped the body, and the tide washed it out to sea?" JD suggested.

I shrugged.

Farther down the beach, the wreckage of a 30 foot sailboat sat amid the dunes. There were still damaged boats scattered all across the island from the hurricane. I jogged down the beach and waved to Sheriff Daniels as I passed.

He gave me a curious glance.

I reached the damaged vessel and climbed aboard. The smell slapped me in the face the minute I pushed into the cabin. The odor hit my nostrils like a wet, moldy sock. It wasn't the first time I'd smelled death, but with the heat and the close quarters, the stench was especially pungent. Flies buzzed about the corpse of a young girl.

It was a horrific sight.

I yelled for the others, and within moments the team join me aboard the abandoned vessel.

Sheriff Daniels grumbled when he saw the body. "Just when I think I've seen everything."

He shook his head.

"That's some twisted shit," JD muttered.

2

Gruesome.

Grisly.

The decapitated body lay in the cabin with a carved pumpkin in place of the head. The hands had been amputated. *Trick or Treat* was carved into the girl's stomach.

Halloween was just around the corner.

Blinding camera flashes flickered throughout the cabin as the forensics photographer documented the crime scene. Brenda, the medical examiner, hovered over the body.

The girl's skin had a pale greenish color. Almost translucent. The bluish veins under the skin were just barely visible.

A tense scowl twisted on the sheriff's steely face. "I want every inch of this boat dusted for prints."

"You know he wore gloves," I said. "He's not stupid."

"Everybody makes mistakes. When he does, we'll nail his ass."

Sheriff Daniels climbed out of the cabin. It wasn't pretty below deck, and I was ready to get out of there myself. I joined him on the beach, and by that time Reagan, and her camera crew, had descended upon the scene.

There was no keeping her away from a story.

"What part of *this beach is closed* do you not understand?" Daniels asked in a gruff tone.

"Have you ID'd the victim yet?" Reagan said, ignoring him.

Daniels glared at her.

"No," I said.

"Do you think it's Abigail Monroe?"

Abigail Monroe had been reported missing several days earlier. I was pretty sure these were her remains.

"I see no need to speculate at this time," Daniels said.

"Can you describe the condition of the body?"

Sheriff Daniels arched an eyebrow at the morbid question.

"Is this one like the others?" Reagan continued.

"I'm not discussing the details of this case until we have a positive ID and the next of kin have been notified," Sheriff Daniels said.

Reagan's blue eyes glanced to mine.

I shrugged. "What *he* said."

Reagan gave me a sideways glance.

JD and I walked with Sheriff Daniels toward the parking lot.

"Please tell me you're not fucking her," Daniels grumbled.

"No," I said, dismissively. "She's totally not my type."

"Every woman with a pulse is your type," Daniels replied.

"That's not true. I have very discerning tastes."

"Excuse me. Let me rephrase that. Every hot woman with a pulse."

I shrugged, innocently. "And your point is...?"

He continued to admonish me. "I just don't want her finding out information that she shouldn't."

"I don't tell her anything that we haven't released to the public. But she's tenacious. She has a way of digging up information."

"Well, maybe she can dig up the identity of our killer. I'm taking a lot of flak over this. This kind of shit doesn't win elections. It drives tourism down."

"And it really sucks for the innocent victims," JD added, dryly.

The sheriff's eyes narrowed at him. "I don't care how you two do it, but get this guy off the streets."

JD and I exchanged a curious glance.

"Does that mean we can use any and all available methods?" JD asked with a devious grin.

"*Legal* methods."

JD frowned. "The killer doesn't play by the rules, why should we?"

"When have you two ever played by the rules?"

The sheriff climbed into his patrol car and tore out of the parking lot.

"I'm hungry," JD said. "Do you want to grab an early lunch?"

"How can you eat after this?"

JD shrugged. "I certainly wasn't going to eat before. That smell was enough to make me want to puke up yesterday's meal."

He looked back to the crime scene. Reagan and her crew were still filming the outside of the vessel, and the investigative reporter went live, broadcasting to her legions of loyal followers.

JD leaned in and muttered, "Are you sure there's nothing going on between you two?"

"Our relationship is strictly professional," I assured.

Jack arched a skeptical eyebrow.

"I'd tell you," I said. "Maybe."

He still wasn't convinced. "Well, if you haven't hooked up with her yet, you're losing your touch."

"Apparently so," I said.

I climbed on the bike and followed Jack to *Taco Loco.* They had some of the best fajitas on the island. And their margaritas were stout. With a hint of *Everclear*, they could creep up on you quickly.

The walls were painted yellow and teal, with red accents. Small sombreros served as lampshades. The walls were adorned with handcrafted items and memorabilia—old highway signs, decorative armadillos made of scrap sheet metal, papier mâché iguanas.

JD and I split an order of beef fajitas. They were sirloin and came with an abundance of guacamole, cheese, sour cream, grilled onions, refried beans, rice, and a creamy garlic butter sauce. I didn't want to know how many calories were in the meal. I figured I'd run them off later.

JD and I scarfed down our bounty like we hadn't eaten in months.

"I'm mad at you," JD said, in a half serious tone.

My face crinkled. "What the hell did I do?"

"This is all your fault."

"It would be nice to know what *this* is."

"You put that bug in her head."

My eyes narrowed. "What bug?"

I had a pretty good idea of what he was talking about.

"The acting bug. Scarlett's up my ass to go to Los Angeles now."

I raised my hands, innocently. "I had nothing to do with that. She asked *me* if I could help her out."

"Yeah, but you didn't actually have to do it," JD said, flatly. "Now she's running around thinking she's going to be a movie star. That's the last thing she needs. I can barely keep that girl under control as it is. What am I going to do when she's 2000 miles across the country? I can't go out there and babysit her. And there is way more trouble to get into in Los Angeles than there is here."

"I'm not so sure about that."

JD loaded up a chip with refried beans, guacamole, and cheese, then stuffed it in his mouth. He mumbled over the crunching chip. "Well, on the bright side, she'd be getting away from this *Sandcastle* thing."

I smiled. "See. It's not all bad."

JD’s skeptical eyes blazed into me. "If she falls off the wagon out there, I’m blaming you."

I rolled my eyes.

"She's got a meeting with her probation officer set up to see if he will clear the trip," JD said.

"Shouldn’t be a problem. She's going out there for employment opportunities."

"I don't know if I'd call it an employment opportunity," JD said, loading up another chip. "Do you know what the statistics are? Do you know how tough it is to make a living as an actor?"

"I know the odds are slim."

"Less than 3% of union actors make over $600 a year. Let that sink in. You pay almost half that in union dues. $350 a year isn't going to cover her coffee bill."

"Joel is one of the best agents in town,” I said. “She's already ahead of the game."

"Do you know what rent is like in that city?" Jack asked.

"Not as bad as San Francisco."

"And then there are the earthquakes. I've got to worry about earthquakes. On top of all the other shit she could get into, I have to worry about the ground opening up and swallowing her."

"She'll be fine," I assured. "You're more likely to die riding a bicycle than you are in an earthquake."

I could see he was more than a little frazzled.

"I told her I'm taking 10% of her earnings. *Stress tax,"* JD grumbled.

I chuckled. "They all have to fly the coop sometime."

JD gave me a sideways glance, then he looked at his watch. "Is it happy hour yet?"

3

Madison slid an envelope across the bar counter. Her blue eyes were full of excitement.

“What’s this?” I asked.

"The results of my ultrasound."

I had stopped in *Diver Down* on the way back to the boat.

The envelope was sealed. "Do you know?"

Madison shook her head. "I'm debating. I kind of want it to be a surprise. And I kind of want to know. I mean, there are a lot of advantages to knowing in advance. I could start decorating and buying clothes." She paused. "I'm not sure what to do. I'm going to think about it for a while. You can look if you want to."

I thought about it for a long moment. "I'll wait until you make a decision."

"Give it to me," Harlan grumbled. "I want to know."

Madison scowled at him. "Sorry, Harlan. You'll spill the beans."

Harlan feigned offense. "I am a vault. I'll have you know that I had top secret clearance in my day."

"Well, this is above top-secret," Madison said, snatching away the envelope before Harlan could get his hands on it.

Madison's ex had gone back to his wife. Madison was all on her own. It was for the best. Ryan was a scumbag. I had caught him cheating with a hottie in a club on Oyster Avenue. Commitment was a fluid concept in Ryan's mind.

I left the bar and strolled down the dock to the *Wild Tide.* My phone rang as I stepped into the cockpit of the boat. It was Big Tony.

"Alright, here's the deal. I got a message to Salvador Zamora. He is considering it. I'll let you know if he decides to meet with you."

"Is there anything I can do to persuade him?"

"It's out of your hands. Just sit back and wait."

I sighed. "I appreciate your effort. Thanks for getting in touch with him."

"It was nothing. Just a few phone calls."

I hung up with Tony, then I stepped into the salon. I was greeted by an overly enthusiastic Jack Russell Terrier bouncing up and down like a kangaroo, barking with excitement.

"Hey, boy. How are you doing?" I knelt down and petted Buddy.

He wagged his tail looked at me with those adorable brown eyes, and if he could talk, he would have said, "Let's go for a run!"

It wasn't a bad idea.

I leashed him, and within moments, we were trotting down the dock toward the parking lot, his paws clattering against the wooden planks.

We did a short 3-mile loop. I was drenched in sweat by the time I made it back to the *Wild Tide.* The sun blazed high overhead.

JD called. "Brenda has identified the victim. Just as you suspected. Abigail Monroe. The victim has evidence of a previous fracture in her left fibula that matches Abigail's past x-rays. Belinda's running DNA for confirmation."

I cringed.

I knew the moment Abigail went missing it was trouble. Her family had posted signs all across the island—in restaurants, bars, hardware stores, you name it. The xeroxed image of Abigail's smiling face was emblazoned on my retinas. Every time I saw her picture, I dreaded the day we'd find her body. I hated that my thoughts drifted to the worst possible outcome. But as long as the *Sandcastle Killer* was out there, more girls would go missing.

"Daniels wants us at the station ASAP."

"Has the family been notified?"

"Well, sort of."

"What do you mean, *sort of?*"

“Daniels wanted to wait until the DNA evidence came back, but the victim’s mother saw the story on the news, and she is at the station demanding to see the remains."

I cringed. “I’ll be right there.”

There was no time to take a shower. I toweled off, pulled on a clean shirt, then jumped on the X6. I was at the station in a few minutes.

4

"I have a right to see my daughter," Tina, Abigail's mother, demanded. Her shrill voice echoed throughout the station.

Sheriff Daniels tried, and failed miserably, to calm the grieving woman. "Ma'am, we haven't finished our testing."

"I know it's her! I want to see her." Her eyes were red and puffy, mascara had stained her cheeks. She had short blonde hair, was mid 40s, and was carrying around a little more weight than she probably would have liked.

"Ma'am, I have to warn you, the victim's remains are—"

Tina cut him off. "Her name is Abigail. And stop calling me *ma'am.* You can call me Tina or Ms. Monroe."

Sheriff Daniels frowned. A heavy sigh escaped his lips. "I can have my deputies escort you to the medical examiner's office."

"Thank you."

Daniels glanced to JD and me. It was our cue to take over.

"Ms. Monroe, I'm Deputy Wild. This is Deputy Donovan. We are investigating the case. I know this is a difficult time. I thought we might ask you a few questions before we head over to the medical examiner's office."

"I told the deputies everything when I reported her missing."

"Maybe there is a small detail that could be useful."

I motioned to the conference room, and we stepped inside. We took a seat at the oval-shaped mahogany table, and the overhead florescent lights made the room feel harsh and sterile. JD closed the door so we could have some privacy.

"You two don't look like deputies," Tina said, eyeing us suspiciously.

"We sometimes work undercover," JD replied. "Think of us like a special task force."

She gave him a skeptical glance through bleary eyes. "Like I told the other deputies, the last time I had contact with her, she told me she was on the way to work."

"And where is that?" I asked.

"I didn't like it, but she was a cocktail waitress at *Forbidden Fruit."* Then she made certain we understood, "She was just waitressing. Abigail was very modest, and she would never... expose herself... in that kind of way." Tina's lip crinkled with disgust. It was clear she didn't approve of Abigail's line of work, nor the establishment itself.

"Did you two have any disagreements?"

Her face tensed. "Well, typical mother/daughter stuff. But nothing serious."

"Like what?"

"Well, I wanted her to find another job. I wanted her to go back to school. I didn't like the crowd she was running with. Those *bar* people stay out all hours of the night and drink way too much." She paused. "I don't want you to think we didn't have a good relationship."

"I don't," I said.

"You don't think I had anything to do with her going missing, do you?"

I shook my head. "Can you give me a list of some of her friends?"

"Sure."

"When did you report her missing?" JD asked.

"She usually got off work late—2 AM, and by the time she got out of the club, it was usually 3 AM. Then sometimes she'd go to an after-hours club with friends. We talked every day. When I didn't hear from her the next evening, I began to get worried. She had just moved out and gotten her own apartment a few months ago."

"Does she have a roommate?" I asked.

Tina nodded. "Sarah Dodson."

"Did Abigail have a boyfriend?"

"I don't think so. She broke up with Brad maybe six months ago."

"Did she date around a lot?"

Tina's eyes narrowed at me, clearly offended. "Was she promiscuous?"

"That's not what I asked."

"Abigail was very... She didn't sleep around."

"I'm just trying to determine if there were new people coming in and out of her life."

"Sure," Tina said. "She was meeting people all the time. That's what people of that age do."

"Did she ever mention to you that she felt unsafe?"

"No."

"What about Brad? How did their relationship end?"

Tina shrugged. "I don't really know. She didn't give me a lot of details. I think it just kind of fizzled out."

"Do you know if he was upset about the breakup?"

"Why are you asking these questions? There is a serial killer running around this island. Isn't that where you should be focusing your attention?"

"We are," I said. "I'd just like to rule out any other possibilities and get a sense if she may have had contact with the killer in a social setting."

"I'm done answering questions. Take me to see my daughter." Her eyes welled, and tears streamed down her cheeks.

5

The color drained from Tina's face when she saw her daughter's body on the metal slab. The place smelled of death and chemicals. Stark white walls were offset by stainless steel counters and washbasins. There were biohazard waste containers, purple nitrile gloves, beakers, test tubes, electron microscopes, centrifuges, and an array of stainless steel surgical items. There were several stainless steel autopsy tables in the room with hydraulic lifts. Blood gutters in the tables allowed fluids to drain. It was a macabre sight that belonged in a haunted house or a horror movie.

Tina's knees wobbled, and JD and I caught her before she smacked the tile floor in the autopsy room. She came to a few moments later, and JD and I helped her to a couch in a nearby hallway.

She sobbed uncontrollably.

JD found some tissues and brought her bottled water.

"That's definitely her," Tina said between jerking sobs.

"I promise, we'll get the person who did this," I said.

Tina wasn't in any condition to drive home. JD drove her car, and I followed them in the red Porsche. As we dropped her off, I assured her once again that we would find the person responsible, but that did little to console her.

JD and I switched places, and he took the wheel behind the convertible. "Where to?"

"I say we talk to the roommate, then we go pay a visit to Jaco."

JD was never one to turn down an opportunity to visit *Forbidden Fruit.*

We drove across town to the *Oceanside Apartments* where Abigail had lived with her roommate Sarah. The modest apartment complex was nowhere near the beach, and certainly not ocean-side. There were multiple buildings that contained four apartments each—two up, two down. Sarah lived on a second floor walk up, apartment #209.

We banged on the door and a soft voice filtered through, "Who is it?"

I held my gold badge up to the peephole. "Coconut County Sheriff."

"Come back with a warrant," she shouted.

JD and I exchanged a glance.

"We just want to talk to you about Abigail."

There was a long moment of silence.

Then the deadbolt unlatched, and Sarah pulled open the

door. She was a pretty young girl, about 21. She had straight dark hair, blue eyes, and a svelte body.

"I don't really know anything," she said. "She was here one day and gone the next."

"We're just looking for any additional details that might help us connect the dots," I said. "Can we come inside?"

"I don't let cops in my house without a warrant."

"You have something to hide?" JD asked.

The brunette scowled at him. "No. I'm just exercising my constitutional rights."

"Fair enough," I said. "We're not the bad guys. I promise."

She rolled her eyes.

"When was the last time you saw Abigail?" I asked.

She shrugged. "I guess it was the day she went missing."

"When was that?"

"I don't know. Don't you already know this stuff?"

"I only know what I've been told. Your recollection may differ from that of someone else. It's important we get a broad overview of the situation."

"I think it was a Thursday," Sarah said. "But don't hold me to that. My days all run together."

"How did you meet Abigail?" JD asked.

"At the club. We worked together. We got along, so we decided to become roommates."

"So, you're a cocktail waitress at *Forbidden Fruit?"*

She scoffed. "No. I'm a performer."

"What about Abigail?"

"She danced too."

JD and I exchanged a curious glance.

"So, she wasn't a cocktail waitress?" I asked.

Sarah rolled her eyes again. "No. That's just what she told her mother."

"See, we are learning new information," I said. "Her mother said she was on her way to work the night of her disappearance."

"I guess," Sarah said. "I had gone shopping that afternoon. I'm not sure if she was planning on going into the club that night or not."

"What did she like to do in her free time?" I asked.

Sarah shrugged. "I don't know. What does anybody like to do? I mean, we go to the beach sometimes. Shopping. Drinking. If we weren't working, we were out at the clubs, or on dates."

"Was she dating anybody specific?"

"Nobody in particular," Sarah said. "We are hot young girls. Why limit ourselves to just one guy? These bodies aren't going to last forever, might as well have a little fun with them before they get old and saggy."

The way Sarah described Abigail was nothing like the way her mother did.

"Did you know any of her boyfriends?"

"I can barely keep up with mine."

"What type of guys did she like to date?" I asked.

Sarah looked at me, hesitantly. "Well, guys our age are total losers. They're broke, immature, and they last about two seconds in bed."

"So, she liked older men?"

"Older, *rich* men," Sarah clarified.

"What about you?" JD asked with a hopeful smile. "Do you like older rich men?"

Sarah groaned. "You are so not my type."

JD deflated.

"Would you recognize any of these men?" I asked.

"I didn't meet most of them."

"She didn't bring anyone to the apartment?" I asked.

"It wasn't that kind of arrangement."

I could tell she was holding something back. "What kind of arrangement was it?"

Sarah was silent for a long moment. Then she spilled the beans. "I'm not gonna get in trouble for this, am I? I mean, you can't arrest me for anything I say, can you?"

6

"You're not a suspect," I said. "If you know something that could help the investigation, please tell us."

Sarah hesitated. "Abigail had *arrangements* with several men."

"Financial arrangements?" I asked.

Sarah nodded.

"So, she was a prostitute?" JD asked.

Sarah's face twisted. "No. It wasn't like that."

"What was it like?" I asked.

"She had men that would do her favors in exchange for..." Sarah's voice trailed off, not wanting to spell it out.

"Sex?" I asked.

Sarah nodded.

"Sounds like a prostitute to me," JD muttered.

Sarah glared at him. "She was not a hooker!"

"You say tomato, I say *tomato*."

"How did she find her clients?" I asked. "The club?"

"Sometimes. But half the guys that come in there don't have two nickels to rub together. They blow their whole paycheck on a few dances, and expect a blow job for 100 bucks," Sarah said. “The guys that *do* have money are great, but you have to tip out to the house. It cuts into the profit margin. Plus, sleeping with a guy in the club makes me feel dirty.”

JD and I exchanged a glance.

“Makes *you* feel dirty?” JD asked.

She sighed, then conceded. “Okay, so, I may have exchanged a few *favors* in the club. But I don’t do it on the regular. It’s gross.”

"Where did Abigail meet most of these men?" I asked.

"Online. There's a website that facilitates connections between older wealthy men, and young, available women. Maybe you need someone to pay your car payment? You can work something out. Maybe you want your rent covered? There will be someone willing to do it."

"For a price," I added.

Sarah nodded.

"I take it you use the website as well?" JD asked.

Sarah's eyes narrowed at him. "Like I said, you’re not my type."

"You girls make good money at the club without doing extras," I said. "Why would you need to do that?"

"Typically, the men that we meet through the site are more generous, and more refined. You can specify exactly the terms your interested in. You have complete control. Some of them are even cute."

"You wouldn't happen to have access to Abigail's account, would you?" I asked.

Sarah shook her head.

"What's the name of the site?"

She told me, and I scribbled the URL down on a piece of paper.

"Do you think the killer is finding victims through that website?" Sarah asked, concerned.

I shrugged. "It's a possibility. If you have any other friends that are utilizing that site, I'd warned them to be extremely cautious."

Fear bathed her eyes.

"If you can think of anything else that might be helpful, please get in touch," I said.

Sarah said she would. She closed the door and latched the deadbolt as JD and I strolled to the parking lot.

"She paints a very different picture of Abigail, doesn't she?" JD said.

"Indeed."

"I say we get access to Abigail's profile on the site and check her private messages," JD said.

"We'll need a warrant for that."

"Or, you might be able to call in a favor," JD said with a sly grin.

I knew what he was getting at. "I don't know how many more favors I can pull out of Isabella."

"Don't sell yourself short. I'm sure you could charm a few more out of her."

We hopped into JD's Porsche and drove to Oyster Avenue. We parked at a meter and strolled down the sidewalk to the strip club. Music thumped inside the dim den of debauchery. Colored lights slashed the foggy air. Exotic beauties in stiletto heels pranced on stage, slinking around chrome poles.

It was a feast for the eyes.

Much to JD's chagrin, we were a little too early for happy hour.

We scanned the club, looking for Jaco, the manager.

I wouldn't go so far as to call us regulars, but we were no strangers to *Forbidden Fruit.*

Jaco saw us and strolled in our direction. "I take it this isn't a social call?"

"How can you tell?" JD asked.

"You both have that look in your eyes. You're not here for fun."

“I have fun wherever I go,” JD boasted.

“I don’t doubt that,” Jaco replied.

"Tell us about Abigail Monroe," I said.

"She the dead girl you found on *Surfside Beach?*"

I nodded.

Jaco frowned and shook his head. "That's too bad. I liked her. Customers did too."

"Did you see her the night she went missing?"

Jaco shook his head. "I think she worked the day before."

"Are these girls on any type of set schedule?" I asked.

"Not really. They come and go as they please. Some of the more professional girls treat this like a business and come in on certain days. That way the regulars know when they can find them."

"Do you think you could give me a list of Abigail's regular customers?" I asked.

Jaco looked at me blankly. "No. We value discretion around here. How long do you think this place would stay open if my customers thought their name would end up on a list that was given to law enforcement? It's the reason I don't have security cameras. Half the guys that come in here are married. You think they want their wives finding out?"

"I don't know if you've been keeping up with the news, but there's a bad man out there doing bad things to young girls," I said.

"And it breaks my heart. It really does. But to tell you the truth, I don't keep track of these people. I don't know who her regular customers were. You can ask some of the other girls. I doubt they were paying attention to Abigail's regulars." Jaco paused. "Did you talk to her roommate? Sarah?"

"Yeah."

"She probably knows as much as anybody." Jaco put a friendly hand on my shoulder. "Look around. Have a good time. Do what you gotta do. Drinks are on the house. You gotta pay for the girls, though. I wish I could be more helpful."

"Thanks, Jaco," JD said.

Jaco turned away and headed back toward the bar.

"Oh, hey, Jaco. One more thing," I said. "Do you know anything about this website? The one that facilitates *introductions?*"

Jaco leaned in and muttered. "I got nothing to do with that website, if that's what you're asking. I run a legitimate business here. If the girls want to provide *extra* services, that's between them and the client. I make money off the door and the drinks."

"They don't have to tip out to the house?" I asked.

"They pay a flat fee to come in and work. And there's a mandatory tip out to the house on earnings above that. From there, I dispense a portion of that to the bar and waitstaff." He paused. "I am not a pimp. How they make their money is solely up to them. And I don't want to know how they do it."

"Relax, Jaco," JD said. "Nobody's coming after you."

"Just so we're on the same page," Jaco said.

"We're on the same page," JD assured.

"Do you know how hard it is to run a business like this and keep everything aboveboard?" Jaco asked. "I got people coming in and leaning on me all the time. The fire marshal. The city health inspector. Vice cops. The mob. Everybody's got their fucking hand out."

"Not us, Jaco," I said.

A sly grin curled on his lips. "And that's why I like you two." His grin turned into a full smile. "Like I said, drinks are on the house. And please, don't connect this establishment with that sicko out there. That's not good for business. I'm just now rebounding from the last incident here."

A gorgeous girl strutted toward me and draped her luscious form around me. Her sultry voice tickled my ear. "Hey, cutie. I'm mad at you!"

She frowned and turned out her bottom lip.

Jaco chuckled. "I'll leave you to your investigation."

7

I stared at the gorgeous brunette, wondering what I had done to draw her anger. She had flawless skin like porcelain, green eyes, sculpted cheekbones, and red lips that could entice a man to commit murder.

"I gave you my number, and you never called," she pouted.

I had no recollection of her whatsoever. And with a face like that, I would remember. I fumbled for an answer. "I must have misplaced it."

"A likely story," she said, doubtful. Her green eyes smoldered. "You don't even remember me, do you?"

"No. I totally remember you."

"What's my name?"

"Your real name, or your stage name?"

"I only tell my real name to men I like."

JD watched the exchange with amusement.

I tried to hide my inner turmoil as I racked my brain, trying to remember the stunning beauty. Had I killed that many brain cells? Was this early onset dementia? Hell, I was barely into my 30s.

I stalled for time. "I bet you don't even remember *my* name."

Her eyes narrowed at me. She knew exactly what I was doing. "I guess I just wasn't that memorable."

She spun around and pretended to walk away.

I grabbed her hand. "Not so fast."

A sassy smirk curled on her full lips.

It was the moment of truth. I had to at least make a guess. You miss 100% of the shots you don't take. I stammered, "Your name is..." I thought of something outrageous. "Griselda. "

She arched a curious eyebrow. "Do I look like a *Griselda*?"

"Gertrude?"

Her face twisted.

"Hildegard?"

"Okay, smart ass."

"I have no idea what your name is, sorry."

She chuckled. "It's okay, I'm just messing with you. We never met. I thought you were cute and wanted to harass you."

"Feel free to harass me anytime," I said.

"So, how about a dance?" she asked.

"I see. It's all about the Benjamins."

"A girl's gotta make a living."

"I guess I could make a donation to your college fund," I said.

She laughed again and took my hand and led me to a secluded chair. I glanced back at JD who gave me the thumbs up.

$100 later, and I still didn't know her real name.

She was a good entrepreneur. I had to give her that. But she left me all wound up with nowhere to go.

We weren't getting much police work done, so JD and I left the club. We stepped onto the sidewalk, and the harsh sunlight turned my eyes into tiny slits. It took a moment to adjust to the wash of light.

I decided it was time to call Isabella and ask for another favor. She was my former handler at the most powerful clandestine agency in the world. *Cobra Company.* A completely independent and unaccountable entity that did the dirty work the three letter agencies didn't want to do.

"What is it this time, Tyson?" Isabella asked.

"I got Cartwright off the books for you. That ought to count for something?"

"It does, which is why I am entertaining your request."

"I need you to hack into a website."

"Where is the server located, and what is the security level?"

"Unknown." I gave her the URL. "I need all the private

messages from a specific profile. The victim may have had contact with the *Sandcastle Killer."*

"You're chasing down serial killers now?"

"Always in the pursuit of truth and justice."

Isabella chuckled. "What's the username?"

"I don't know. I'm sure she used a false identity. Her real name was Abigail Monroe. I can send you an image. Perhaps you can do a facial recognition search with the user profiles and get a user ID."

I texted her a picture of Abigail after we hung up. Isabella said she'd let me know as soon as she had something.

We strolled down the sidewalk and climbed into JD's Porsche. He grumbled about a parking ticket that fluttered in the breeze underneath the wiper blade, pinched against the glass. He grabbed it and crumpled it up. "Now that's some bullshit. We are five minutes past the timer!"

"Just go down to the courthouse, flash your badge, and use your charm. We were here on official County business."

We climbed into the car, and JD cranked up the flat six. The engine howled as he revved it. He dropped it into gear and pulled away from the curb, launching into traffic.

With the music blaring, we raced across town to *Diver Down.*

“What will it be, boys,” Madison asked as we strolled to the bar.

We took a seat next to Harlan.

JD and I each ordered a beer, and we bought one for Harlan.

Madison drew a bottle opener from her back pocket, spun it around, and popped the tops off three long necks faster than a hummingbird in action. The amber bottles hissed, and she slid them across the counter, dripping with condensation.

Harlan lifted the bottle and tipped the neck and said, "Much obliged, gentlemen."

The salty old Marine was a regular at *Diver Down.*

"I saw Reagan's report on the news," Madison said with concerned eyes. "Were you able to ID the victim?"

I nodded.

"How worried should I be? This whole thing has me freaked out."

"Just relax. I don't think you're in the killer's target demographic."

"What do you mean?"

"He's targeting a specific group of girls. They're all about the same age and have the same appearance."

"Yeah, they're all young and hot," JD muttered.

Madison's eyes narrowed at him. "I'm young and hot."

"Well, the *young* train is leaving the station," JD muttered under his breath.

Madison's eyes narrowed at him. "I'm 25, dick!"

"That's like 72 in bikini model years," JD teased.

Madison smacked him with a wet washcloth she'd been using to mop up the bar.

He tried to shield the blow. "Hey, easy there!"

"If I'm old, you're a fossil," Madison barked.

"Age is all in the mind. I identify as a 22-year-old."

Madison rolled her eyes. "You're as old as dinosaur bones. I'm going to start calling you DB."

JD's face twisted. "That's awfully close to *douche bag."*

Madison shrugged. "If the shoe fits..."

JD frowned at her.

"Seriously, though," Madison said to me. "How worried should I be?"

"Well, I think you should maintain good situational awareness. You shouldn't work the bar alone. You need to always have someone with you when you take the trash out or go to the parking lot. And I think you need to be armed."

"Believe me, I'm packing." She pulled a compact 9mm from underneath the bar and brandished the weapon.

"I think that will take care of you," I said.

She stowed the weapon away. "I hate that I have to even think about this stuff. This is crazy. What happened to this island? It used to be so safe. What has gotten into people? I mean, what kind of wires have to get crossed for somebody to enjoy hacking up someone?"

"It's a sick world," JD muttered.

"This isn't public knowledge, so keep it between us," I said. "The victim was a sex worker. She used a certain website to arrange liaisons. There's a possibility that's how the killer is acquiring his victims."

"What website?" Madison asked, her eyes wide with curiosity.

I told her the URL. "I shouldn't really be saying anything yet."

"Mums the word," Madison said, zipping her lips.

I took another sip of my beer, then my phone rang. It was Sheriff Daniels. "What's up, boss?"

His grim voice crackled through the tiny speaker on my phone. "We have another situation."

8

"We've got another missing person," Daniels said.

I grimaced. "Let me guess... College-age? Attractive? Female?"

"Natalie Watson. 21. Blonde hair, blue eyes. 5'2".

"When was the last time anyone saw her?"

"Last night. Her friends say she left a bar with a guy, and they haven't seen or heard from her since."

"Maybe they're still shacked up? We're not even talking 24 hours yet?"

"Yeah, well, in light of the current circumstances, her family is really spooked. The sooner we can get on this, the better. If she miraculously shows up, then no harm, no foul."

"Roger that," I said. "Do we know who this guy is that she left the bar with?"

"Her mother is down here at the station, along with the two

girls that were with her last night. I've got an artist working on a sketch of the guy. You two need to get down here ASAP."

"Copy that."

JD paid the tab, and we zipped over to the station. We were there in less than 10 minutes.

Sheriff Daniels scowled at us as we strolled into the lobby. His nose twisted as we got close to him. "You two smell like beer and cheap perfume. What the hell have you been doing?"

"Investigating," JD said.

Sheriff Daniels pulled a pack of gum from his pocket and offered each of us a stick.

I snatched a piece and peeled off the foil wrapper. Minty flavor filled my mouth.

"Try not to drink on the job," Daniels said.

"We were off duty," JD replied, innocently.

Daniels shook his head.

He led us down the hallway. We greeted Natalie's mother, Gail, and Natalie's two friends, Tonya and Casey, in the conference room.

Daniels introduced us.

Lana, a sketch artist, drew on an iPad, taking notes from the two girls. She had a matte screen protector on the tablet which gave the digital pencil a nice feel as she dragged it across the screen. She made it look effortless.

Gail trembled, and her nervous eyes darted about as she fidgeted. "Please tell me my daughter is going to be okay? Tell me that sick bastard doesn't have her?"

“She could just be out and about and not checking in,” I suggested.

"Natalie usually calls me every day. She’s not picking up her phone. It goes straight to voicemail. This is not like her."

"I understand, and we will do everything in our power to see your daughter’s safe return," I said. "It's still early. And the more we know, the better chance we have of finding her before something happens."

The color drained from Gail's face.

Lana displayed the sketch to the girls. "Is this him?"

"Make his nose a little thinner. And his lips a little fuller," Tonya said.

“No, his nose was fatter,” Casey protested.

Tonya was a bottle blond with brown eyes, and a serious tan. Her French manicure was in desperate need of a touch up. Casey had auburn hair, light blue eyes, and heavy liner.

Lana spun the pad back around and made a few adjustments. "How's this?"

Tonya and Casey exchanged a look.

"That's him," Tonya said.

Casey's face crinkled. "You think?"

“That’s totally him.”

Casey shook her head. Then sighed. “I mean, maybe.”

“Bitch, you need to get your eyes checked."

Casey scowled at her.

"Do you know his name?" I asked.

The girls consulted one another.

"It started with a D, didn't it?" Casey said. Then she waffled. “I'm not sure.”

"No, it started with a C. Or maybe a K," Tonya said.

"No. I'm pretty sure it started with a D. Like Deke, or Derek, or..."

"No. That doesn't sound right at all," Tonya said.

The two girls bickered amongst themselves for a moment, then Casey looked at me. "I don't know. We were pretty shit-faced."

Casey's eyes flicked to Gail. "Sorry, Ms. W."

If they couldn't remember the man's name, I wondered how accurate their description of him was. "What can you tell me about this guy who remains nameless?"

"He was hot!" Tonya said.

"He was *okay*," Casey countered.

"I would have...” Tonya started in a lustful tone. Then she caught herself “Never mind.”

Her sheepish eyes flicked to Gail.

"Had you ever seen this guy before?” I asked. “Did Natalie know him?"

Both girls shook their heads.

"Natalie just met him that night," Casey said.

"Where were you at?"

"We started at *Reefers*. Then we bounced to *Bahama Jack's*.

And we ended up at *Bob's Barnacle,* where we met psycho-boy."

"How old would you say this guy is?" I asked.

"28, 29?" Tonya said.

"No way. He was 31, maybe 32," Casey countered again.

"No, he wasn't that old."

JD and I exchanged a glance. I'd be surprised if these girls could tell me what day of the week it was.

"Okay. So, he was between 28 and 32 years old. How tall?" I asked.

"5'9"," Casey said.

"6'2"," Tonya overrode.

The two girls glared at each other.

This went on *ad nauseam* with just about every detail regarding the man's appearance. They couldn't agree on anything. I thanked them for their time, took their contact information, and assured Gail we would do everything possible to find her daughter.

Lana sent the sketch of the man to my phone.

It wasn't much to go on, but it was better than nothing.

"Let's go have some chow, then head over to *Bob's Barnacle* and see if any of the bar staff remembers seeing that guy," JD said.

We left the station and drove to Oyster Avenue.

We stopped at *Snorkel* for a bite to eat. The walls were embedded with large aquariums. Colorful fish swam around fake coral reefs. Caustic light patterns were projected on the ceiling, giving the restaurant an underwater vibe. As you can imagine, they served fresh fish and seafood.

We ordered the fried calamari to start. Then decided on a seafood platter to nibble on—stuffed shrimp, stuffed crab, fried fish. We washed it all down with a beer, then headed over to *Bob's Barnicle.*

The *Barnicle* was a laid-back beach bar that served beer, wine, and spirits, along with crawfish, crab, and fried fish entrées. The walls were decorated to look like the hull of a wooden boat. There were large barnacles everywhere, and life preservers hung from the walls. The deck outside was home to a second bar and a small stage for live bands. You could expect to hear everything from reggae to rock'n roll. But the night was young, and the band hadn't taken the stage yet. The crowd was pretty thin at this point.

There were several flatscreen TVs around the establishment. It was a good place to grab a beer and watch a game.

JD and I strolled toward the bar, hoping to find someone who remembered seeing Natalie Watson and the man she left with.

What I saw on the TV behind the bar disturbed me. My blood boiled. *Someone was going to get a stern talking to.*

9

"The body of a local woman has been identified as Abigail Monroe. Her remains were discovered earlier today near Surfside Beach, and she is believed to be a victim of the *Sandcastle Killer,*" Reagan said. "Sources close to the investigation say the woman was a sex worker and used an online service to facilitate illicit relationships. Police believe that the killer may be using this website to select victims."

The URL flashed on the screen.

"Caution is advised for anyone currently using the site."

I clenched my jaw as Reagan continued her mini exposé.

JD gave me an *I told you so* glance. "You've got nobody to blame but yourself. Should have kept your mouth shut."

"I thought Madison knew better," I said.

"Maybe Reagan got her information elsewhere?" Jack said with a shrug. "You know that woman has sources everywhere."

I tried to contain my anger.

We leaned against the bar, and JD flagged down the bartender. He flashed his shiny gold badge. "We'd like to ask you a few questions."

I pulled out my phone and showed him the sketch Lana had created. "Do you recognize this man? He was here last night. Left the club with a petite blonde girl."

The bartender pulled my phone close and examined it.

He was a big guy—6'2", lots of muscles. Short brown hair. Chiseled features. I'm sure he did pretty well with the ladies, working in a place like this.

He shook his head. "I don't know. He's not a regular. I see so many faces come through here, they all blur together. What did he do?"

"The girl he was with is missing."

The bartender's eyes widened. "No shit? Like, you think he abducted her?"

I shrugged.

"Is this connected to the *Sandcastle* thing?"

"I can't discuss ongoing investigations."

He almost looked excited. "Holy shit! That means the killer could have been in this bar. What a trip!"

JD and I exchanged a glance.

"Do you think he'll come back?"

"If he does, call us immediately."

"This is so cool. I mean, it's not cool, but... Wow!"

"Wow," I said in a sarcastic tone.

"Do you have any surveillance cameras?" JD asked.

"No. We had them up for a little while, but the employees, and some of the patrons, complained. People like their privacy. And it made the staff feel like they weren't trusted."

We lingered in the bar and talked to a few of the waitresses, but nobody remembered seeing the man, or Natalie.

JD glanced at his watch. It was almost 7 o'clock. "I'm gonna run you back to *Diver Down*. I've got plans this evening."

"Hot date?"

"29. Redhead. Athletic trainer. Can you say fun times?" JD smiled from ear to ear.

We left the *Barnacle,* found the Porsche, and drove back to the marina. JD promised to give me a full report on the evening's activities. I climbed out of the convertible and strolled into *Diver Down,* the howl of the flat six echoing as JD screeched out of the parking lot.

My body tensed as I strolled inside, and my cheeks flushed with anger. I tried to contain myself. I didn't want to erupt and go overboard. But I intended to give Madison an earful.

I took a seat at the bar and forced a smile.

Madison sauntered over to me. "What can I get you?"

"Well, you can explain to me why you divulged confidential information?" I folded my arms, leaned back, and waited for an answer.

Her face twisted. "What are you talking about?"

"Reagan's report. It was full of confidential information that I only told you."

Her jaw dropped, and guilt washed over her face. "Oh, shit. I'm sorry. I wasn't thinking. She came in for a drink and we just got to chatting and... fuck!" She sighed.

"You have to be careful around her. It's not just girl talk. She's like a sponge and will soak up anything you say."

Madison huffed. "That's kind of shitty."

"She's a reporter, Madison. Not your friend."

"She *is* my friend. I like her. I just thought we were speaking in confidence."

I shook my head.

"I'm really sorry. It won't happen again. I promise."

"You're right. Because I'm not sharing any more details with you."

She scowled at me. She started to protest, then relented. "You're right. It was totally my fault. You told me something in confidence and I let it slip."

I remained silent for a moment.

"How can I make it up to you?"

I scratched my chin and pondered her offer for a moment. "I don't know. I'll think of something."

She grabbed a beer from a bucket of ice, popped the top,

and slid it across the counter to me. "This one's on the house."

I gave her a nod of thanks and sipped the cold beer.

I hesitated, then pulled my phone from my pocket and showed Madison the picture of the sketch. "Have you ever seen this guy before?"

She studied it carefully. "No. I mean, it's really hard to tell from a sketch."

The phone buzzed, and Isabella's number flashed on the caller ID.

"Excuse me. I gotta take this." I swiped the screen. "What have you got?"

"You're not going to like it."

"Lay it on me."

"The website is based in Russia. It's using a high level of encryption. I can't crack it."

"You can crack anything."

"It's a new encryption scheme. And I don't have the man hours it would take to hack this specific site." Isabella sighed. "Sorry, time is money."

"How long would it take?"

"Something this sophisticated? A couple supercomputers cranking away... maybe never. Not possible with brute force. I'd need to place an operative inside the organization and acquire access through the error of human assets."

"Seems like overkill for a site that is involved in prostitution."

"I'm sure the encryption was stolen from somewhere else. And whoever is running the site doesn't want anyone snooping around." She paused. "I was, however, able to find a profile match with the picture you gave me. So, Abigail Monroe *was* using the site."

I deflated. "Alright. I appreciate the help."

"Anytime. Just remember, I may need something from you." She hung up.

I made my way back to the *Wild Tide* and took Buddy for a walk. The little Jack Russell Terrier was full of energy. I still hadn't found a foster home for Fluffy, and I had a sneaking suspicion that the aloof little animal would become a permanent resident. She and Buddy got along well, and she was surprisingly low-maintenance.

By the time I got back to the boat, Reagan was on board. We had a clash of opinions in the salon.

10

"You need to clear things with me before you broadcast to the world," I said.

Reagan's brow knitted. "You're not the boss of me."

I expected nothing less from the sassy news reporter.

"You could jeopardize the investigation."

She scoffed. "Please. People need to know. They have a right to know. I have a right to tell them. My broadcast tonight could save countless lives."

"If I don't feel like I can trust you with information, I may not share."

She sneered at me. "And I might not share *my* information with you." She paused. "Besides, why are you getting so bent out of shape? You told Madison something. Madison told me. How was I supposed to know you didn't want me to blab about it?"

"First of all, that was shared in confidence. And B,... I don't know what B is, but I'll think of something."

A thin smirk tugged at Reagan's plump lips. "Face it. We need each other."

That hung in the air for a moment. We tried to ignore the sexual undertones.

"I mean, you can help me, and I can help you. And you know that. I can get information out to the public that you need disseminated. If we play our cards right, we can draw this guy out."

"You watch too much TV."

Reagan rolled her eyes. "What about the missing girl?"

I played dumb. "What missing girl?"

She stared at me, flatly. "Natalie Watson."

"How do you find out about this stuff?"

"You can't keep anything from me," she said with confidence.

"If you have other sources, what do you need me for?"

Reagan shrugged. "Well, you're my *best* source."

She batted her eyelashes and tried to make herself look adorable. She didn't have to try too hard.

"Please, do you think that's going to work on me?"

She sauntered close and looked up at me with her big eyes. With a sinfully pouty voice she said, "Aw, don't be mad at me, Daddy."

Her gorgeous eyes, breathy voice, and enticing lips could tempt even the most chaste.

"Do we have an understanding?" I asked.

"What kind of understanding?"

"You know what kind of understanding."

She huffed. "Fine. I will run my broadcasts through you beforehand. Deal?"

"Deal."

"I reserve the right to do whatever I want," she muttered. "But I will run them by you."

My eyes narrowed at her.

"Stop being so uptight. It's not good for your health."

"If stressful shit would stop happening around here, I wouldn't be so uptight."

"Aw." She strolled around behind me and began massaging my shoulders. My traps were tight, and her thumbs digging into my muscles felt sublime.

"Is this your idea of a bribe in order to get me to talk?" I asked.

"Just shut up and enjoy it."

It wasn't a bad idea.

"Relax, let it happen," she whispered in my ear, teasing.

"You are pure evil."

"I know."

I could sense her diabolical smile.

"So tell me about Natalie Watson." She kept stroking my shoulders.

I told her the details that were pretty much common knowledge. Then I mentioned the sketch.

"Let me see it. We could put that on air and get that out to as many people as possible. You might draw some leads."

I pulled my phone from my pocket and launched the sketch. Once I handed the phone to Reagan, my massage ended. Her eyes were glued to the screen. They widened with recognition. "Oh my God. That looks like..."

11

"It can't be," Reagan said.

I could tell she didn't want it to be a familiar face.

"Who?" I asked.

"It sort of looks like Elijah. I mean, it can't be him, though."

"Why do you say that?"

"No way. Elijah is not the type of person that's capable of this kind of thing."

"That's what everybody always says about serial killers."

Reagan shook her head. "There's a vague resemblance here. That's all. This is a sketch. It could be anybody."

"I think we should look into the guy. Elijah cracked the ciphers faster than anyone else. He fits the profile. White male. Early 30s. Socially awkward."

"Why do you think he's socially awkward?"

"How would you describe Elijah?"

She thought about it for a moment. "Socially awkward." Then she emphatically said, "But he didn't do it. I know Elijah."

"Maybe you don't know him as well as you think you do?"

Reagan frowned.

"I've got an idea."

The investigative reporter arched a curious eyebrow.

"I'll come up with a fake note. You can slip it to Elijah and gauge his reaction. If he's the killer, he'll know right away it's fake. He'll be dismissive, defensive, and maybe even angry."

"And if he's not the killer? He's going to be pissed if he finds out we suspected him. It could ruin our professional relationship."

I shrugged. "This business is all about tough choices."

Reagan was silent for a long moment, then finally exhaled. "Okay, fine. I'll go along with this. But if he's innocent, and he ends up hating me, it's all your fault."

"And if we catch a killer?"

"Then I'll take credit on the evening news." She smiled.

At least she was honest.

I spent the rest of the evening fabricating a note that resembled the other letters Reagan had received from the killer. I used the same kind of paper, a cipher that was similar, and even went so far as to prick my finger to stain the message with blood.

"I think we should give this to Elijah tomorrow," I said.

Reagan agreed. She thought about it for a moment. "And what if he gives us a reaction indicative of a killer?"

"Then we follow him around and see if he's up to anything," I said. "I'll have Denise run a background check. See if there's anything in his history that might indicate the potential for violence."

"I really feel weird about setting up a coworker like this."

"Get over it. I didn't think you had that much of a conscience?"

Reagan looked shocked and offended by my comment. "I'm not a sociopath," she gasped. "Just because I'm driven, aggressive, and career oriented doesn't mean I don't have feelings."

I raised my hands in surrender. "I didn't say you didn't have feelings. I'm sure there's a kind, caring person under that tough exterior."

"A girl has got to look out for herself in this business."

"I don't doubt it."

"I may seem cold and callous, but I can be very caring and compassionate toward the people I love." She paused. "I just don't have time for bullshit and drama. I don't let a lot of people in." She thought about it for a moment. "We're not really that different, you and I. You're focused and driven. You don't suffer fools well. You certainly don't wear your emotions on your sleeve. But I've watched you. You'll do anything to help someone. Especially the people you care about. Hell, you let me stay here, and you didn't know me from Adam."

I shrugged. "What can I say. I'm a sucker for hot, sassy reporters."

She sneered at me playfully. "You're not a bad guy, Tyson. But don't worry, I won't tell anyone that."

"You better not. I can't have you go ruining my reputation."

She chuckled. "Oh, you have quite the reputation. I don't think I could ruin it."

I arched a curious eyebrow at her.

"You've discharged your weapon more than anyone else on the force. And I'm not just talking about your 9mm. You notoriously chase anything with a skirt. And there are things about your past that even I can't find out. And I can find out just about anything."

"Still trying to dig up dirt on me?"

"You are an enigma, Tyson Wild." There was a tone of flirty admiration in her voice. She looked away and muttered, "And Lord knows, you've been completely appropriate with me. I guess I must not be your type."

She flicked her blue eyes to me, batted her lashes, and her pupils dilated slightly.

I knew that look. I'd seen it before.

She backtracked. "Did you say, hot?"

"Have you been drinking? You're awfully complementary."

Her sultry look quickly turned into a scowl. She smacked my arm. "No. I have not been drinking. Not excessively. I had a glass of wine earlier. Not like last time." Her eyes went wide as she realized her slip up.

"So, you remember?"

"Remember what?" she asked innocently, knowing damn good and well she had thrown herself at me when she was inebriated.

We had both pretended the incident didn't occur.

Reagan stepped closer. "Can't a girl give a guy a compliment?"

Someone turned up the heat in the salon. Energy radiated from her body. Her sultry voice tickled my ear, went straight to my spine, traveled south, and increased blood flow in a certain area. My heart beat faster. "What happened to keeping things professional?"

"Nothing wrong with one professional appreciating another?"

She moved closer still.

"*Appreciating*, eh?"

"Don't you want me to appreciate you?" The question was so loaded, it was about to pop.

I could appreciate her all night long, and the next morning too.

Our lips were like two trains speeding down the same track on an inevitable collision course. It was a crash that I was highly anticipating. I grabbed the small of her back and pulled her body into mine. Her body felt warm and supple. She lifted up on her tiptoes, and a subtle whimper escaped her lips as they parted.

This was probably a bad idea, but there was no stopping

what was already in motion. It had been brewing for a long time. We were both sober, and of clear mind. *As clear as either of our minds could get in the midst of surging hormones.*

Our lips were millimeters apart when my phone rang.

"Ignore it," she whispered.

I cringed. "I gotta take it. It could be the sheriff."

“Fuck the sheriff.” Her husky voice was full of desire.

12

"Tyson, you need to come quick," Scarlett said. Her terrified voice crackled through the tiny speaker on my phone.

"What's going on?"

"It's dad. I think he's having a heart attack."

Scarlett almost never called Jack *Dad*. I knew it was serious.

"Call 911. I'll be right there."

"Hurry!" she cried.

I hung up the phone, stuffed it in my pocket, and bolted toward the hatch. I grabbed my helmet on the way out. "Sorry. Can I get a rain check?"

"What is it?" Reagan asked.

"Jack just had a heart attack!"

Reagan's eyes widened with concern. "I'm going with you."

"Grab a helmet."

She looked at me like I was crazy. "Oh, no! I am not riding on that thing with you."

Reagan grabbed her purse from the counter and pulled out her keys. "I'm driving."

We stormed into the cockpit, and I helped her down to the dock. Reagan's high heels clacked against the wood planks as we jogged to the parking lot. We hopped into her car, and I gave her directions to JD's house. The tires spit gravel as we peeled out of the parking lot and raced across the island.

The short drive felt like an eternity. My stomach twisted, and my nerves buzzed. The sinking feeling in my gut was accentuated when we turned the corner and I saw the flashing red and white lights of the ambulance flickering across Jack's house. The strobes left spots in my eyes.

We pulled to the curb, and I bolted out of the car and dashed up the driveway. The front door was ajar, and I pushed into the foyer not knowing what I'd find. I worried that he'd be dead on the floor.

The EMTs had JD strapped onto a yellow gurney and were preparing to load him into the ambulance. A nasal cannula provided extra oxygen.

It was a depressing sight, but at least he was still breathing.

Jack had a scowl on his face. "Would you tell these people I'm fine?"

"What happened?" I asked.

"Nothing happened. Scarlett's being overly dramatic. She's practicing for her acting career."

"I am not being dramatic. You were the one who said it felt like an elephant was standing on your chest."

"He complained of chest pain, dizziness, heart palpitations," an EMT said. "His vitals are fairly normal. Heartbeat is elevated. BP is high. Oxygen saturation was a little low. We started him on O2. Based on his EKG, we need to bring him in."

"I feel fine now," JD said, putting on a cheery face. "This is ridiculous."

"Sorry, Mr. Donovan," the EMT said. "We don't mess around with heart conditions."

"I don't have a heart condition!" Jack declared.

"If you complain of chest pain and dizziness, you're taking a ride in the wagon. No two ways about it." The EMT was adamant.

JD put on a good front, but I could see the fear in his eyes. I was worried about my friend.

"Where is the news crew?" JD asked Reagan. "This is newsworthy, isn't it? *One of Coconut Key's finest suffers near fatal heart attack?"*

"I thought you were feeling fine?" Reagan asked, dryly.

"I am, but that makes for a more dramatic headline, doesn't it—since we're all being dramatic?" His glare snapped to Scarlett.

"Excuse me for wanting to keep you around a little longer," Scarlett sassed.

The EMT addressed Scarlett. "Do you want to ride with us, or take your own car?"

"I'll ride with you," Scarlett said.

JD frowned, then begged me for assistance. "Would you talk to these people?"

I shrugged. "It sounds like you need to get checked out."

"I've got plans tonight. This is screwing up my whole evening."

"Yeah, well, you don't want to screw up your whole life, do you?" Scarlett asked.

JD grumbled to himself as the EMTs wheeled him out of the house. They opened the doors to the ambulance and loaded him inside. Scarlett climbed in behind him. Before the EMTs closed the doors, I told her we would meet them at the ER.

Reagan and I jogged to her car and hopped in. She cranked up the engine, dropped the car into gear, and we followed the ambulance to the hospital, staying close behind as it pushed through red lights. Cars pulled to the curb getting out of the way. Lights flickered, and the siren wailed.

At the emergency room, JD was triaged immediately. *They take care of you right away when you come in via the meat wagon.* The triage nurse checked his vitals again, gave him another EKG, and asked a slew of questions.

Of course, Jack flirted with her.

He was taken back to a room, and we tagged along. The nurse gave him a green hospital gown with diamond patterns on it. “Put this on, opening to the back.”

"Do I really need to wear this?"

"Yes," the nurse said. "You do."

JD frowned, then looked to us. "A little privacy?"

We stepped out of the room while JD changed, and the nurse let us know when we could come back in.

Another nurse put electrodes on his chest and attached an oxygen saturation monitor to his finger. The display by the bed blipped with each beat of JD's heart, making a craggy mountain range on the screen. With a blood pressure cuff around his arm, his BP was displayed on the monitor in real-time.

Jack winced as the nurse jabbed a needle into his vein and started IV fluids.

"The doctor will be in to see you shortly. Press this button if you need anything," she said.

"I *need* to get out of here," JD groaned.

She chuckled as she left the room.

JD glared at us as we took seats beside the bed. "I'm telling you, I'm fine."

"Let's leave that call to the professionals," I said.

The nurse had folded his clothes and put them on the counter. Jack pointed to the pile. "Grab my cell phone from my pants pocket, would you?"

I stood up, walked across the pale green room, and fumbled through the pockets. There were cabinets and drawers full of medicine and surgical instruments. There was a stainless steel wash station with a pump bottle of antibiotic hand scrub. A box of blue nitrile gloves sat atop the counter near packages of gauze and a red bio-hazard container.

I tossed the phone to Jack. "What are you going to do? Order a pizza?"

"I need to call my date and tell her I'm not going to make it."

I took a seat while he dialed the number.

"Hey, doll," Jack said in a hopeful tone.

He didn't get very far before the woman's angry voice crackled through the speaker—loud enough for us all to hear.

"Just hold your horses," Jack protested. "I know I'm late, but a situation came up."

I think I heard his date say, "You better be dead or in the hospital."

"Well I'm not dead."

"Yet," she replied.

"I'm in the ER."

"Seriously?"

"Seriously!"

"Oh, my God. Are you alright? What happened?"

"Well, I was thinking of you, and I got a little excited. They think I may have had a heart attack."

"Are you fucking with me?"

"No, I'm serious," JD said. "If you don't believe me, come here and see for yourself."

"I like older men, but not ones that might die on me during sex."

Jack's eyes perked up. "So, you're saying I was going to get lucky tonight?"

"If you played your cards right. But, apparently, you got dealt a bad hand."

"Don't worry, I'd live long enough to finish." JD winked.

"Jack!" Scarlett exclaimed. "Hello? I'm in the room. Could you not talk about that stuff in front of me?"

Jack covered the phone and muttered, "Don't listen to my conversation."

It was hard to tell who was the parent in this situation.

The doctor pushed into the room wearing a white lab coat with a stethoscope around his neck. He smiled and said, "Good evening. I'm Dr. Parker. What seems to be the trouble?"

"I gotta go," JD mumbled into the phone. "I'll call you back if I don't die."

13

The doctor asked Jack the same questions that the triage nurse and EMTs did. He looked at JD's vitals on the monitor, then leaned over the bed and listened to Jack's chest with his stethoscope.

The doctor seemed unimpressed, then stood tall. "Your EKG looked a little funky, but nothing too abnormal. I want to get a CT scan, chest x-ray, and some blood work. Someone from radiology will be in shortly."

"I promise, I feel fine," JD said.

"Better safe than sorry." Dr. Parker smiled and slipped out of the room.

15 minutes later, a radiology tech stopped by and took JD to get his scans.

I waited in the room, with Reagan and Scarlett, for Jack to return.

"I hope he's okay," Scarlett said with worried eyes.

"JD is a tank. Nothing can hurt him," I said, hoping it was true. I tried to change the subject. "How did it go with your probation officer?"

"He says I can go to Los Angeles," Scarlett said, emotionless.

Under normal circumstances she would have been ecstatic. Now she just slumped in her chair.

"That's good news."

"I guess."

"Having second thoughts?" I asked.

"What if Jack's really sick? I can't leave him now."

"I'm sure this is nothing."

"What if it's not?" She looked at me with terrified eyes.

"Don't go there just yet."

Jack was back in the room within 15 minutes, but it took another hour to get the results of the CT and the labs.

During that time, Carol, JD's date, showed up. She wore leather pants and a leopard-print tube top. Her pretty face was covered with a tad too much makeup, and her blonde hair wasn't entirely natural. JD wasn't lying. She had abs you could bounce a quarter off of. The girl was in shape. Muscle cuts in her arms, legs, and calves. Not an ounce of fat anywhere.

"I'm shocked," Carol said. "I thought you were totally full of shit."

"Would I ever lie to you?" JD said with a grin.

Her eyes narrowed at him. "I haven't made up my mind yet."

JD made introductions.

Carol smiled at Scarlett. "I've heard so much about you."

"I haven't heard anything about you," Scarlett replied in a snotty, disinterested voice.

There was an uncomfortable silence.

Carol forced a smile and changed the subject. She looked at JD. "So, how long are they keeping you? I hope this is nothing serious."

JD shrugged. "I'm still waiting on the test results."

"Oh, shit!" Reagan muttered to herself as she checked her phone.

"What is it?" I asked.

Her eyes widened as she scrolled through her feed on social media.

"Small crisis," she said, underplaying the situation. "I'll be right back."

She stood up and moved into the hallway.

Dr. Parker stepped into the room a few minutes later, looking over JD's chart. "No AFIB. No SVT. No intracranial hemorrhaging. Chest x-ray looks clear. I don't think there's anything to be concerned about. I'm going to call this paroxysmal tachycardia."

JD's face crinkled. "What the hell does that mean?"

"It means you have a high heart rate. Have you started any new medications? Are you under any abnormal stress?"

JD shook his head. "There's nothing abnormal about my stress level. Same old shit."

"I'd say everyone's normal stress level is too high," Dr. Parker said.

"He is coming off of opioids," I added.

JD glared at me.

Dr. Parker arched a curious eyebrow. "And what were you on the opioids for?"

"Pain management from a gunshot wound."

"Gunshot wound?" Dr. Parker seemed both surprised and impressed. He looked over the chart again. "I see here you are a deputy sheriff, is that correct?"

"Yes, sir!" JD said, proudly.

"That's a high stress occupation."

"It pales in comparison to raising a teenage daughter."

Scarlett's eyes narrowed at him.

"Elevated heartbeat could be associated with opioid withdrawal. Possibly you had some type of panic attack. I'm going to admit you to the cardiac care unit for 24 hours—just for observation. That way we can monitor your heart rhythm through the night and see if there's anything unusual going on. If there are no issues, you will be discharged sometime tomorrow. Then I want you to follow up with a cardiologist and take it from there."

"Do you have to admit me?" JD asked.

"You can do whatever you want. But if you leave the ER, it would be against my professional advice."

"I feel great. I think this is all nonsense," JD said.

"You're staying," Scarlett demanded. Her eyes blazed into him.

"You're not the boss of me," JD said.

Scarlett huffed and folded her arms.

"Jack, I think it would make Scarlett feel better if you stayed," Carol said.

"It would make *me* feel better if I left."

"You're not going to get a rain check on our date if you don't stay."

That shut JD up. "Check me in, Doc!"

14

nurse came in to transfer JD to the cardiac care unit. She rolled his bed out of the room and into the hallway.

"I'll stay with him tonight," Carol said. "I'll make sure he behaves."

"Are you sure?" Scarlett asked.

"You go home and get some rest. I don't mind. I've never had a first date in a hospital before. It could be fun."

Scarlett's face twisted with skepticism. "Don't have *too* much fun."

Carol smiled. "I'll keep him in line."

Reagan was still on the phone, doing damage control. She finally wrapped up the call, and we said our goodbyes to JD and Carol, then left the ER.

As we walked through the parking lot, Scarlett broke down. Tears streamed down her cheeks. The pale green glow from an overhead lamp cast long shadows on her face as she sobbed amid the sea of cars in the parking lot. She had kept it together up until now, but the dam broke.

Reagan put her arm around her. "It's going to be okay."

"I know," Scarlett said, wiping her eyes. "I've just never seen him like that before. It scared the shit out of me."

I think it was the first time Scarlett realized JD wasn't going to be around forever. He had a long way to go, but this was a friendly tap on the shoulder from the Universe. A reminder that no one gets out alive.

Scarlett pulled herself together and we climbed into Reagan's car. Scarlett's mascara was smudged, and her nose was red and puffy.

Reagan's phone kept blowing up with texts and calls. She ignored them while she drove.

"Is everything alright?" I asked.

"Not really."

"What's going on? Or do I even want to know?"

She let out a frustrated exhale. "It's ridiculous. I'm getting a ton of flack from my broadcast earlier. The outrage on the Internet is insane. All I said was that the victim, Abigail Monroe, was a sex worker and she was using a particular website. Apparently her family didn't like me referring to her as a prostitute. And there is a legion of keyboard warriors accusing me of victim shaming. My boss wants me to issue an apology."

I rolled my eyes. "This will blow over by tomorrow. People have the attention span of gnats."

"I hope you're right."

We pulled into JD's driveway.

"Are you sure you're going to be okay alone tonight?" I asked Scarlett.

"Yeah. I'll be fine. Thanks for everything."

"No problem. You call me if you need anything."

She gave me a mock salute and hopped out of the car.

We sat in the driveway, and I watched her get inside safely.

"I don't know about you, but I need a drink," Reagan said.

We drove back to *Diver Down* and took a seat at the bar.

"Two shots of tequila," Reagan said.

I arched an eyebrow at her. "Tequila?"

"What's the matter? Don't think you can keep up?"

Those were fighting words. "I have no problem keeping up."

Madison grabbed two shot glasses and rimmed them with salt. Then she pulled a bottle from the well, spun it around, and filled the two glasses with poor life choices. She slid them across the bar with two limes.

We clinked glasses and tipped the shots back. It was smooth, but it still burned. It warmed my body and brought back memories of over indulgences.

Reagan slammed the empty glass on the bar with a clank and said, "Hit us again!"

Madison had barely filled the glass when Reagan tipped it

back again. She let out a satisfying gasp and slammed the glass down. "Uno mass, por favor."

"Maybe you should slow down?"

She looked at me flatly. "Nonsense."

The 11 o'clock news came on the television behind the bar. Reagan cringed as the anchor said, "Good evening. Earlier today, one of our reporters made inappropriate statements based on unverified information. Reagan MacKenzie mistakenly identified a victim of the *Sandcastle Killer* as a sex worker. The statements made by Ms. Mackenzie do not reflect the views of this station or our parent network. Ms. MacKenzie has been suspended pending disciplinary review. In other news..."

Reagan practically spit out her tequila. "I think we're going to need the whole bottle."

Madison poured another round.

I motioned to her to take it easy.

"Last one," Madison said.

Reagan scowled at her.

"That's three shots in four minutes. Why don't you let that settle in for a minute?"

"You are a party pooper!" Reagan exclaimed.

"You'll thank me in the morning." Madison smiled and drifted to other customers.

"This is such fucking bullshit."

Reagan's phone kept ringing, and she kept ignoring it. It lit up every few moments with social media notifications and texts.

"You tell the truth, and people hate you for it," Reagan said.

"You know, if you would have talked to me before you made those remarks, maybe—"

Her eyes burned into me like lasers. "No. You don't get to say *I told you so*. I am a very upset woman. Tread carefully."

I raised my hands in surrender.

"What the hell am I going to do?"

"I don't know. Go on TV and make an apology?"

"For what? There is a little thing called journalistic integrity. I'm not one of these people who plays fast and loose with the facts. I got into this line of work because I wanted to bring the truth to light. What I said on air may not be pleasant, but it might keep an innocent girl from getting killed. I didn't defame anyone. I didn't slander anyone. I just relayed the facts."

Reagan's phone buzzed again and she looked at the display. A grimace twisted her face. "I gotta take this."

She swiped the screen. "So, this is how it goes down? I find out about this on air?"

"Just take a vacation," a voice filtered through her phone. "You could use the time off. Get out of this city. We can talk about bringing you back when things die down."

"I can't believe you're suspending me. Am I at least getting paid during the suspension?"

"You're not getting suspended," her boss said.

There was a long pause.

Reagan's jaw dropped. "You're firing me?"

"I don't know if I'd put it so harshly."

"How would you put it?"

"I'm terminating our relationship."

"You know what, Harold. Fuck you, you spineless dick!" Reagan hung up the phone and slapped it on the counter.

She sighed, and her head fell in her hands. Reagan stayed silent for a long moment. Then she finally surfaced and took a deep breath. "At least I got to tell him to go fuck himself."

"It's the simple pleasures."

"Speaking of pleasure," Reagan said. A naughty glint flickered in her eyes. "I'm super stressed out right now. My body is tense all over. I'm very, very tight."

Her breathy words slid from her satin tongue and hung in the air for a moment.

"Do you think there's anything you can do to help me relax?"

"I can think of a few things," I said, trying not to sound too eager.

"And would one of those things involve..." She leaned in, and her hot breath tickled my ear. She said something that got my full attention. In no uncertain terms, she told me exactly what she wanted me to do to her.

She put a delicate hand on my knee and stroked my thigh.

I had every intention of indulging her desires. I paid the tab, and we nonchalantly left the bar. I didn't want to telegraph what we were about to go do, but I think it was pretty obvious.

I held the door for her and we stepped outside, heady with lustful thoughts. At first I didn't pay attention to the man that stepped out of a black SUV.

Then he called me by name.

15

"Mr. Wild?" the man asked.

He was a thick guy with dark hair and a goatee. He wore a suit and a black shirt underneath. I could see his shoulder holster and the semi-automatic pistol that it contained.

"Mr. Zamora would like to meet with you."

"Now?" I asked.

The man nodded. "It's a one-time offer, and Mr. Zamora doesn't like to be kept waiting."

I'd been angling for this meeting for a long time, and I wasn't about to pass it up. But that didn't mean I wasn't conflicted about it.

Reagan had a confused look on her face.

"I need to go," I muttered. "Can we pick this up later?"

Her face crinkled, and she looked offended. "You're going to pass up this to go with him?"

"It's important."

"And I'm not?"

"I didn't say that."

She flashed me a sassy look. "Your loss. This was a one-time offer too," she said, pointing to her hot little body as she backed away from me.

She spun around and sauntered down the dock toward the *Wild Tide,* putting an extra sway in her hips just to rub it in.

I exchanged a glance with the man, and there was a small degree of sympathy in his eyes. "You must really want to talk to Salvador?"

"You could say that."

"No weapons."

I figured as much. I didn't like it, but it was the terms of the meeting. I lifted my shirt and carefully pulled my holster from inside my waistband and handed the weapon to the man.

He took it from me and said, "You'll get this back after the meeting."

Then he motioned for me to spin around while I held my shirt up.

"I need to frisk you."

"Whatever floats your boat."

He patted my cargo shorts down, and when he was satisfied, he motioned me toward the SUV.

I climbed into the backseat and slid across the smooth leather. I buckled my safety belt, and the man climbed in beside me.

There was a driver and a passenger up front. Both of them were armed.

"What's your name?" I asked the man beside me.

I don't think he wanted to tell me.

"Call me Roderigo."

"Tyson," I said, extending my hand. I figured I would at least be cordial.

He stared at my outstretched hand and declined my offer.

Roderigo pulled the door shut and nodded to the driver. The SUV cruised out of the parking lot and whisked me to a palatial estate on the other side of the island. We pulled into a driveway, beyond wrought-iron gates, that opened automatically. We followed the drive and circled around to the front of the house. The driver parked the car, and Roderigo hopped out and held the door for me.

I thanked him as I stepped from the vehicle.

"This way," he said.

I followed him to the door, and the man in the passenger seat followed behind me. I didn't particularly like being sandwiched between the two thugs, but I desperately needed information from Salvador Zamora. I was willing to do just about anything to get it.

The foyer was tiled with Italian marble, and the dual staircases spiraled up to the second floor. To my left was a parlor with a nice library full of leather-bound editions. At the end of the foyer was the main living area. The home was impeccably decorated with what I would describe as modern classic furniture.

In the living room, Salvador Zamora mixed a drink at the wet bar and dropped in a few cubes of ice with silver tongs. They crackled when they hit the expensive liquor.

Salvador smiled. “Ah, Mr. Wild. So good of you to come. Can I offer you an adult beverage?"

"Sure."

"What's your poison?"

"I'll have what you're having."

“MacMillan X 64. My favorite."

"A man with good taste," I said.

It was an extremely expensive single malt scotch from the Highlands of Scotland. Not something you could buy at your local liquor store.

Salvador was impeccably dressed in a double breasted suit with a cotton broadcloth shirt, tie, and matching pocket square. He had dark, slicked back hair that was graying on the sides. He had an expertly trimmed mustache and goatee. His deep tan, dark eyes, and chilled features made him a hit with the ladies. This was a man who had good taste and enjoyed the finer things in life. He oozed style and sophistication. He didn't strike me as your average drug dealer.

Salvador was smart.

He never handled product himself. Never talked about his business on the phone or in email. From what I could tell, he only gave orders to his trusted associates, who then spread the commands to lower-level thugs on the totem pole.

The Feds could never get anything on him.

It drove them crazy.

He poured me a drink, dropping in a few cubes of ice, and handed me a glass. We toasted, and I sipped the fine whiskey.

It was smooth with a capital S.

"What can I do for you?" He knew damn good and well why I was here. Big Tony had told him everything.

I needed to phrase things carefully. Salvador would never implicate himself in any criminal activity.

“Let me preface this by saying I am here strictly for personal reasons. Not in any official capacity."

"If you were here in an official capacity, we wouldn't be having this meeting."

I smiled. "Some *acquaintances* of yours were killed a few years ago. The weapon used to kill them was the same weapon that was used to kill my parents. I thought, perhaps...“

"...I might be able to shed some light on the situation?" He paused for a moment, giving away nothing.

I wasn't entirely sure he would answer my question.

Then, after an almost unbearable silence, he said, "I have a vague recollection of reading something in the paper about those two men. I wouldn't call them *acquaintances*. It's possible that I met them socially here or there, you understand."

I nodded. I knew they were his employees.

The whole act was bullshit. But I didn't care *how* he told me what happened, as long as he told me. I could read between the lines.

"What I recall, and I could be mistaken, was that those men were shot on the water, and their boat, and whatever it contained, was stolen. Now, there was some speculation about an illicit transaction gone bad. At least, that's what I remember reading in the paper."

"These strangers that you *don't know*... If you had to guess, who do you think may have killed them?"

"I like to fancy myself an armchair detective," Salvador said. "I love mystery novels. I'm fascinated by cold case files. I watch all of those crime shows on the Internet."

"Me too."

"That particular crime went unsolved, but it seemed obvious to me that the authorities should have looked into Esteban Rivera. He was a large trafficker of narcotics at the time."

"At the time? Where is he now?" I asked.

"A few bad decisions, a few enemies made, that kind of thing can make a man go into hiding."

"Any idea where?"

Salvador smiled. “If only I knew. Perhaps he went back to Columbia.”

I suddenly realized why Salvador was helping me. He probably wanted Esteban taken care of.

"Do the initials XC mean anything to you?"

"Trust me,” Salvador said. “That's not who you're looking for."

I regarded him curiously.

"From what I hear, XC is just a low-level guy who deals in stolen merchandise. You want the man XC acquired the boat from. You want Esteban. He may not have pulled the trigger himself. But it was most likely men in his employ.”

"And you're certain about that?"

Salvador smiled. "I'm not certain about anything. This is all hearsay and conjecture. The ramblings of a crazy old man with a failing memory and a penchant for mystery novels."

Salvador Zamora wasn't old, his memory wasn't failing, and judging by the leather bound classics that lined the bookshelves in the parlor, he was well read.

"I appreciate your time and generosity."

We shook hands, and I swallowed the rest of the expensive whiskey. "Thanks for the drink."

"My pleasure. And I trust we will never meet again. Especially in a professional capacity."

16

Disappointment didn't even begin to describe the way I felt when I returned to the boat. Reagan was passed out in the guest room. So much for indulging desires.

I took Buddy for a walk to burn off some energy, then I filled his bowl with water and made my way to the master suite. When I woke up the next morning, Reagan was already gone.

I made breakfast—an omelet with cheese, mushrooms, onions, and spinach. After taking Buddy out, I took a shower, got dressed, then grabbed my helmet and strolled down the dock toward *Diver Down.* It was a beautiful morning. There was a cool breeze coming off the water and not a cloud in the sky. The boats gently swayed in their slips.

I breathed in the fresh air. Despite the chaos, there was nowhere in the world I'd rather be.

I pushed into the restaurant and took a seat at the bar. "Have you seen Reagan?"

Madison was getting ready for the day. "Yeah, she stopped by not too long ago. She told me to tell you that she was going to the station to pick up her belongings, and that she would deliver the note to Elijah. Whatever that means?"

"Thanks. Did she say when she'd be back?"

"No." Madison paused. I could tell something was on her mind, but she was hesitant to ask. After a few moments, her curiosity got the best of her. "So, you two looked pretty... close last night. Anything interesting happen?"

"No. And if it did, I wouldn't tell."

Madison rolled her eyes. "Please, you two have had a thing for each other from the beginning."

"I don't know what you're talking about."

"How is Jack?" Madison asked.

"I don't know. I'm about to call him."

"That's pretty scary stuff. I hope he's okay."

"Me too." I dialed Jack's cell phone.

After a few rings, he answered. "Have I got a story for you!"

"I'm all ears."

"Well, you're going to have to wait. My phone is about to die. Can you run by the house, grab my charger, and bring it up here?"

"Sure thing. Do you know when you're getting out?"

"They still have me hooked up to this monitor. I don't think

I'm getting out of here until this afternoon, unless I organize a jailbreak."

"Have you had any more episodes?"

"Define episode? I mean, I certainly had my heart rate elevated last night, if you know what I mean?" Jack said in a lecherous tone.

He started to say something, but the call disconnected. I assumed his battery went dead.

"Looks like I'm Jack's errand boy today," I said to Madison. "I'll catch you later."

I left the bar, pulled my helmet on, put on my gloves, and straddled the crotch rocket. I cranked the engine up and revved the throttle a few times, then eased out the clutch and rolled out of the parking lot, onto the highway.

I was wearing a T-shirt and cargo shorts—not my full race leathers. When I rode like this, I was extra cautious. I had put the bike down once before, and I didn't plan on doing it again. They say there are two kinds of motorcycle riders. *Those that have crashed. And those that will crash.* I hoped that I had gotten my one and *only* crash out of the way on this bike. But there were never any guarantees.

I zipped over to JD's and pulled into the driveway. I knocked on the door, and after 15 minutes of banging, Scarlett answered with an annoyed face. She squinted at me through tired eyes. She had a low, dry, raspy, morning voice. She whined, "What do you want?"

"I need to pick up a few things for Jack. You know where his phone charger is?"

She shrugged. "Feel free to look around. I'm going back to bed."

"What did you do last night after we dropped you off?"

She looked like she could have been hung over, and I worried for a moment that maybe she had gotten into a bottle to drown her anxiety.

"I was too wound up to sleep," she said. "I stayed up watching movies till 4:30 AM."

I *think* she was telling the truth.

Scarlett yawned and stretched like a cat, then wiped the sleep from her eyes.

I rummaged through the house and found Jack's charger. "Do you think he needs anything else?"

"Maybe a fresh change of clothes for when he gets discharged?"

I went into Jack's bedroom and fumbled through the drawers and picked out a pair of shorts, a T-shirt, and a Hawaiian shirt. How could I go wrong with that choice?

"Do you want to go to the hospital with me?" I asked.

"Is he okay?"

"He sounded fine when I talked to him this morning."

"I'll go up there later. I have the keys to Jack's car." She grinned, then spun around and staggered back to her room and fell into bed.

I hopped back on the bike and cruised up to the hospital. A lady at the information desk in the lobby told me where the cardiac care unit was, and I took the elevators up to the 4th floor. Jack was in room C-415.

I strolled through the antiseptic hallway, looking for the room number. The walls were two-toned—sea-foam green on top, mauve on the bottom. There were fake plants in the corners and soothing pastel paintings of seascapes on the walls. The sound of ventilators filtered into the hallway from dim rooms. Death lingered in the shadows.

"Can I help you?" a nurse asked from behind the main station.

"Jack Donovan?"

An exasperated look washed over her face. It was easy to see that Jack had probably been a handful the previous night. This particular nurse was completely over it. She pointed to the room a few steps away.

"Thank you," I said quietly.

I poked my head into the room and saw JD reclining in bed, watching TV. He was still hooked up to the monitors, and his vitals displayed on a screen by the bed.

He looked relieved to see me. "Thank God. I didn't know what I was going to do without a phone."

“There's a phone right there," I said, pointing to the landline by the bed.

"Yeah, but I don't know anybody's number. That's all stored in my *contacts* in my phone."

I found an outlet for the charger and strung the chord to the bed. He plugged in his phone, and a few moments later, it sprang to life with a red charging icon.

I took a seat by the window. "How are you feeling?"

"Fan-fucking-tastic!"

"You look better than you did last night."

"I really think it's a result of coming off the medication. Ever since I stopped taking that stuff, I'm just a little irritable. Sweaty. I get dizzy easy."

"Well, hopefully that's all it is." I paused. "I take it you had a good time last night after we left?"

A look of pure ecstasy filled his face. "Oh, my God, dude! You would not believe it."

I just shook my head.

JD was about to tell me the story when Dr. Parker stepped into the room. "Good morning, gentlemen. How is our patient doing?"

"Top of the world," Jack said.

"Well, we didn't pick up any abnormalities in your heart rhythm last night. Your blood work is fine. I can't really find anything wrong with you. Your heart rate did get a little high during the night for a brief period of time, but from what the nurses tell me, that was due to external stimulus?"

A sheepish grin curled on Jack's face and he shrugged.

"I'd like to keep you here until after lunch—just to give us some more data. If we don't catch anything on the monitor, I'll prepare your discharge papers, and you can go home. But I would like you to follow up with your cardiologist on Monday."

"Will do, Doc," JD said.

Parker left the room. He talked to a nurse in the hallway before moving on.

As soon as he was out of earshot, JD said, "So, get this. At first they were gonna put me in a semi-private room, and I said fuck that. I'll pay extra for a private room. I didn't want to be in with someone snoring all night. So, they finagled it so I could be in here. We're not in the room 15 minutes when Carol says to me, *she's never done it in a hospital before*."

I knew where this story was going before he even started telling it.

"So, I say, *now's your chance.*" JD had a shit-eating grin on his face. "She pulled off that tube top and stripped out of those leather pants, and let me tell you... kapow! That woman is built like a brick shit-house.

"Then she asks, *do you think you're healthy enough for sexual activity?* You're goddamn right I'm healthy enough, and if I'm not, I can't think of a better way to go out.

"So, she saddles up and goes to town. She's bouncing up and down, riding me like a goddamn rodeo queen. The heart monitor is going *beep, beep, beep, beep.* The bed's rattling and bumping into the wall, and I'm just trying to hang on for dear life.

"To top it off, she's a screamer.

"I mean, she's moaning and howling, and I know damn good and well everyone on the floor can hear it. One of the nurses comes in to check and make sure everything is okay, and I think she about had a heart attack when she saw us."

I chuckled.

"Needless to say, you can bring me to the hospital anytime if that shit's gonna happen."

I laughed again.

A commotion in the hallway drew my attention. It sounded like an argument. Voices grew louder and louder. It was unusual for the cardiac care unit. My curiosity drew me to the door, and I peered down the hallway. My face crinkled with confusion at the sight.

17

"You cannot come in here, sweetie," the nurse barked in a condescending tone.

"Excuse me?" Denise said. She stood in the hallway in full uniform.

I rushed down the corridor to see what was going on. "Is there some kind of problem here?"

"I'm sorry, but strippers are not allowed in the hospital. Mr. Donovan cannot have any more visitors!"

Denise looked flabbergasted. "Strippers? You think I'm a stripper?"

The nurse looked her up and down. "You got the body for it."

The nurse had obviously either been on duty last night, or heard about Jack's escapades.

I flashed my shiny gold badge and said, "She really is a deputy sheriff. That isn't a costume. Those aren't tear-away pants."

The nurse looked Denise over again. She forced a smile. "I'm sorry. My mistake."

I took Denise's arm and escorted her down the hallway. Her face was still crinkled with disbelief. "What's going on here?"

"Long story. Jack had a little too much fun last night."

"In the hospital?"

We entered the room.

"Hey, doll," JD said with a smile.

"I thought I'd swing by on my way to work to see how you were doing, but apparently you're doing okay." Denise said.

"You look disappointed. Were you hoping I had died?"

She scowled at him playfully. "No." Denise gave him a hug. "The nurse thought I was a stripper. Can you believe that?"

"No. Who would think that?" JD asked, his voice thick with sarcasm. "I know I would never want to see you naked."

She slapped his arm gently.

JD caught her up to speed on everything that had happened. Well, almost everything. He left out the bit about the Rodeo Queen.

"You know what I could use?" JD said. "A cheeseburger. "Let me tell you, the food here leaves a lot to be desired."

"Do you want me to go grab you something?" I asked.

"Would you? I'm going to be in here past lunch, and I don't think I can eat anymore of the slop they serve."

"Denise, do you want anything?" I asked.

"Oh, no. Thank you. I'm on my way into the station. I just thought I'd stop by for a minute." A thought sparked in her brain. "By the way, I ran the background check that you asked for on Elijah. He's clean. No priors, no history of violence."

"Good to know," I said.

I caught Jack up to speed on all the details about Elijah and the fake note.

"Where do you want the cheeseburger from?" I asked.

Jack thought about it for moment. "Beef Barn."

"Coming right up."

I said goodbye to Denise and strolled down the hallway to the elevator bank. The nurse looked mortified as I passed. "I'm so sorry. I hope I didn't offend that lovely deputy?"

I smiled. "Don't worry about it. If she can put up with us, she can put up with anything."

"Amen to that."

I chuckled and continued to the elevators. My phone rang just as I stepped into the lift. It was Reagan. I swiped the phone and took the call.

"He called me!" her terrified voice said.

"Who called you?"

The elevator doors slid shut and I lost the connection.

I called her back when I stepped into the lobby.

"Who do you think?" Reagan said.

"When?"

"Just now. I don't know how he got my cell phone number. Only my friends and close coworkers have it."

"Does Elijah have it?"

"Yeah, but it's not him."

"Did you give him the note?" I asked.

"He knew it was fake right away."

"That would be an indicator that he might be a suspect," I said.

"It's not him. I guarantee it. He was in the room when the killer called me."

"How do you know it was the actual killer? It could have been anybody. A prank call? Who knows?"

"It was him. I know it. I just got an icky vibe talking to him." Reagan shuddered. "He was using a voice modulator, which only added to the creepy factor."

"It could be somebody yanking your chain."

"He threatened Harold. Called him at home. Told him if he didn't re-hire me, he'd kill him."

"Sounds like you've got a fan. Does that mean you got your job back?"

"Sort of," Reagan said. The killer wants me to interview him. On air. Live."

"Of course he does. He's a narcissist. Or, someone who's

looking to pull one over on the station. Are you going to do it?"

"Hell yes, I'm going to do it. Do you know what the ratings will be for a show like that?"

I grimaced. "Maybe you should ease into this thing. Do a little more research. If this isn't the killer, and it's just some kids pulling a prank, you're going to lose credibility."

"I know he's the killer. He told me where the body of Natalie Watson is."

18

I cringed. "Where?"

"He says the body is tied to an anchor near the reef at Barracuda Key."

"I'll call Sheriff Daniels. When is your next contact with the killer?"

"I told him I would need to check with my boss about the interview, and he said he would call me back."

"Keep me posted. In the meantime, I'm going to verify his story and see if I can trace the call. And I'm not ruling out your buddy, Elijah. He could have had someone else calling you, pretending to be the killer."

"That seems unlikely."

“I'm keeping my mind open to all possibilities."

"I'm getting another call," Reagan said. "I gotta go."

She hung up, and I made an immediate call to the sheriff. I told him I'd meet him at the station.

Then I called Isabella. "I need you to trace a call."

"What's the number?"

I gave her Reagan's cell number and the timeframe of the call.

"I'll call you when I have something." Isabella hung up.

I rushed out of the lobby, found my bike, and raced to the station.

Daniels was ready with the scuba team, the forensics team, and the medical examiner. I boarded the sheriff's patrol boat and we headed toward the reef at Barracuda Key.

The sheriff brought the boat on plane, and we carved across the water. The engines roared, leaving a trail of white water in our wake. Mists of salt water sprayed me in the face as the boat rose and fell with the swells. The wind blew through my hair, whistling my ears.

"Seems like your boy is changing his MO," the sheriff shouted over the rumbling engines.

I shrugged. "Maybe we're going on a wild goose chase? Or maybe he's having second thoughts about brazenly dumping bodies? The reefs are far more secluded."

It took a half hour to get to Barracuda Key. The divers plunged into the water, and bubbles rose to the surface as they descended to the depths.

The boat rocked back and forth atop the water, and I sat on the gunwale, waiting. The sun was high overhead. I didn't have any sunscreen, but fortunately Brenda did. She handed me a tube of SPF 30, and I slathered the creamy white substance on my face, neck, and arms.

"Where's your sidekick?" Brenda asked, snidely.

I told her the situation. Her eyes widened and her jaw dropped. She looked genuinely concerned. "I guess that warrants a phone call, doesn't it?"

I shrugged.

JD hooked up with Brenda once, maybe twice. Things were a little awkward between them after that.

A few moments later, a diver surfaced and shouted, "I found something!"

Sheriff Daniels idled the boat to the diver's position.

I leaned over the gunwale to speak with the diver.

"Another body. Young girl. Missing her head and her hands. She's tied to a Danforth anchor."

I cringed.

"Looks like your reporter is talking to the real deal," Daniels said.

The divers took photographs of the underwater scene, then brought the remains to the surface. They loaded the body onto the patrol boat, and Brenda went to work.

"I won't be able to tell much until I get back to the lab," she said. "Judging by the condition of the body, the victim hasn't been in the water long, but there is likely no usable evidence. The killer has been exceptionally thorough, leaving nothing behind so far. I don't expect that to be any different with this case."

The body was placed into a zippered cadaver bag, and we headed back to the sheriff's office. From there, the body was loaded into the medical examiner's van, and Brenda drove the remains to her office.

"You're going to fill the paperwork out on this one, aren't you?" I asked, hopeful.

Sheriff Daniels scowled at me. "No. That's what I pay you for."

"You don't pay me, remember?" I smiled.

The sheriff's stone face just glowered at me.

"I told JD I'd bring him lunch." I looked at my watch. "I'm already almost 3 hours late."

Sheriff Daniels growled for a moment, then relented. "Go on. Get out of here. But only because numb-nuts is in the hospital."

"Thanks, boss."

I cranked up my bike and headed over to the *Beef Barn* to get Jack a cheeseburger. I decided to get one for myself while I was there. They had great burgers. My favorite was their mushroom cheeseburger with Monterey Jack and Cheddar. I ate mine there and took Jack's to go.

Denise was long gone by the time I made it back to the cardiac care unit, but Scarlett had arrived.

"Where the hell have you been?" JD asked.

I shrugged. "I got sidetracked."

I was hesitant to tell him about the latest victim. I didn't want to put any more stress on him, but he kept prying, so I indulged his curiosity.

Scarlett looked mortified by the story.

"Why didn't you tell me? I could have gone with you."

"I didn't tell you because you need to stay here until you get discharged."

He shook his head dismissively.

I put the styrofoam container on the rolling table next to Jack's bed and positioned it so he could eat. I pulled out a soda from the bag, along with packs of ketchup and mustard.

JD's eyes widened with delight. He took a sip of the soda, and his face twisted at the taste. "There's no alcohol in this."

I rolled my eyes. "How about you wait until you get out of the hospital?"

He gave me a sideways glance then tore into his cheeseburger. He could barely fit his mouth around the hulking piece of beef. One burger was really enough for two people. The meat was pink and juicy and dripping with grease and cheese.

Jack wolfed it down like he hadn't eaten in a month. He licked his fingers when he was done. "Damn, that hit the spot."

It almost felt sacrilegious bringing a cheeseburger into a cardiac care unit. There were people in here dying from clogged arteries, and Jack was doing his best to load his own up with grease. Despite his diet, his cholesterol levels were fine.

Jack was a freak of nature.

I was pretty sure that at the end of the world, there would be cockroaches and Jack. Maybe, he just might outlive the cockroaches?

The nurse stepped into the room with several papers and a manila folder in her hand. "Well, Mr. Donovan. I've got good news, and I've got bad news."

19

"The good news is that I'm getting rid of you," the nurse said. "The bad news is that I met you in the first place."

Jack frowned at her. "I'm not so bad once you get to know me."

"You have been a total pain in my ass since the moment you arrived."

Scarlett laughed. "Try living with him."

"No thank you," the nurse said.

She handed Jack the discharge papers and went over the instructions with him, including the advice to follow up with a cardiologist on Monday.

"Thank you for putting up with me," JD said with a smile, trying to get in her good graces.

She looked at him flatly. "Oh, don't try to be nice now."

She spun around and sauntered out of the room.

"Another day or two, and she'd warm up to me," JD said, confidently.

Scarlett rolled her eyes.

We stepped into the hallway and gave JD some privacy while he got dressed. It was hospital policy that all patients had to be discharged in a wheelchair, so we waited until another nurse was available to take him down to the patient pick up point.

Scarlett got the car from the parking lot and pulled the Porsche around. JD hopped into the passenger seat, and Scarlett drove him home.

I called Reagan as I strolled through the parking lot toward my sport bike. "Did you hear back from the killer?"

"Not yet."

"We found the body of Natalie Watson exactly where he said we would."

"Shit." Reagan sighed. "I was kind of hoping this was all an elaborate prank."

"I'm afraid not."

"Has the victim's family been notified?"

"Sheriff Daniels is handling that. I'm going to head back to the *Wild Tide.* Let me know as soon as you hear anything."

"Any luck tracing the call?" Reagan asked.

"Negative."

"Alright. I'll talk to you later."

I climbed on the bike and cruised back to *Diver Down.* I stopped in and took a seat at the bar.

Harlan was in his usual spot.

"How's JD?" Madison asked.

"Like nothing ever happened."

"That's good. Can I get you anything?"

"Whiskey. Rocks."

"Tough day?"

I sighed. "You could say that."

I was about to tell her about the latest victim when Reagan appeared on the 5 o'clock news.

"Turn this up," I said.

Madison grabbed the remote and raised the volume.

"A young girl's body was discovered near Barracuda Key Island this afternoon. The remains are, as yet, unidentified, but the woman is believed to be the third victim of the *Sandcastle Killer.* We will have an exclusive interview with a man who claims responsibility tonight at 9 PM."

"Oh my God, that's terrible," Madison said. "Is it that girl that went missing a few days ago?"

I nodded. "We don't have a positive ID yet, but the killer told us exactly where to find her. I'm sure it won't take Brenda long to confirm the ID."

"I thought Reagan got fired?" Harlan said.

I shrugged. "Well, you know. Showbiz."

I called Reagan, but it went straight to voicemail.

She called me back 20 minutes later. “It's all set up. He's going to call my cell phone tonight at 9 PM while we are live *on air*.”

"Thanks for giving me a heads up," I said with a twinge of annoyance.

"I'm telling you right now. The killer called just after we hung up. This thing happened faster than I anticipated. Are you sure there's no way you can trace him?"

"I’m working on it. But he's very sophisticated and tech savvy."

"Why don't you come down to the station about 8:30 PM?" Reagan said. "I'll put you on the list."

"I'll be there."

20

I took Buddy for a walk, then grabbed a quick shower, changed clothes, then hopped on my bike and headed to the television station.

I pulled into the parking lot, strolled into the lobby, and checked with security. I was on the list and was given a visitor badge, then escorted through a maze of corridors to the soundstage.

The studio was a large, two-story space. The news set was in the corner of the room. The rest of the walls were painted black so they wouldn't reflect light. Movie lights hung from the grid overhead and illuminated the set. A blue screen behind the anchor desk allowed the editors to composite whatever background they wanted—usually a cityscape of Coconut Key.

There were three large cameras on rolling tripods. Production assistants and crew personnel scampered about.

Reagan saw me as I entered the soundstage and rushed to greet me. "Thanks for coming."

"You bet," I said.

"How do I look?" Reagan asked.

"You look great."

I didn't even need to look her over. She always looked great.

"I'm nervous," she said.

"Don't be nervous. You've done stuff like this thousands of times before."

"I've never done anything like *this*. And a lot of people are going to be watching. The network is pushing the feed out to other markets. Some of the national networks may pick this up."

"The more people that see it, the better. Maybe someone out there can recognize this guy's speech pattern?"

"Has Brenda identified the latest victim's body?"

I nodded. "She matched a tattoo on the victim's skin. The family has been notified."

"So, I can make an announcement on air?"

I nodded.

"I'll show the sketch of the potential suspect. Perhaps someone will recognize him?"

"Where's Elijah?" I hadn't ruled him out as a suspect.

"I'll introduce you," Reagan said. "Be nice."

"I'm always nice."

Reagan looked at me flatly, then waved Elijah over.

He trotted across the studio, and Reagan introduced us. We shook hands, and I sized him up. He *did* resemble the sketch, but the details weren't exact. His nose was a little thicker. And his hair a little curlier. His face was rounder, and he wasn't anywhere close to 6’2”.

I played nice. "Thanks for all your hard work in decoding these messages."

"Anything I can do to help, just let me know." He paused. "Do you think this guy is for real?"

"He certainly knew where we could find the body of Natalie Watson," I said.

"This whole thing creeps me out. I hope you guys catch him."

"Me too."

"It was nice to meet you. I gotta run. We're about to go on air." Elijah spun around and dashed away.

"See, he's harmless," Reagan said.

I gave her a skeptical glance.

"Well, looks like I’m on," Reagan said.

She gave me a hug and a kiss on the cheek, then headed toward the set. A make-up artist applied last-minute touchups to her flawless face, then she took a seat behind the desk.

The evening news anchor, Emma Steele took a seat next to her. She was a gorgeous blonde in her early 30s that had several *enhancements*. Her nose had been done, her chin, and her chest. Lip fillers, collagen injections, and Botox™.

Whoever did the work was good. But you could tell she wasn't all natural, if you knew what to look for.

Crew personnel scampered around at the last minute, then the production manager yelled, "Quiet on the set!"

The rumble of the studio quieted until you could hear a pin drop.

The production manager shouted, "And we're live in three, two..."

"Good evening, I am Emma Steele, and this is a Coconut Key breaking news update. A dark shadow has loomed over our peaceful island for several weeks. A sadistic killer has prayed on innocent victims, committing horrific crimes. Tonight, we have an exclusive interview. Our very own investigative reporter, Reagan MacKenzie, will speak live, on air, with the *Sandcastle Killer."*

I rolled my eyes. Just yesterday, they had disowned Reagan, now they were introducing her like she was their darling.

Emma continued. "We must caution our viewing audience, this is a live broadcast, and the content may be disturbing. Viewer discretion is advised."

"Thank you, Emma," Reagan said. "The *Sandcastle Killer* has been communicating with me for weeks now through encrypted messages. Today, he called me directly. I urged him to stop this reign of terror. Unfortunately, I was too late to save Natalie Watson from a grim fate. The killer directed law enforcement to the remains of her body. Natalie is the latest victim in a slew of killings by this evil man. Natalie was last seen at a bar on Oyster Avenue, *Bob's Barnicle.* She was seen leaving the club with this man."

The sketch flashed on the screen.

"If anyone recognizes this individual, please contact the Coconut Key County Sheriff's Department."

The number to the Sheriff's office flashed on the screen.

"The conversation you are about to hear does not reflect the views of the station, or our parent network. The caller will most likely be modulating his voice, making himself unrecognizable. But if anyone recognizes his speech patterns or phrases, please contact the Sheriff's office."

Reagan placed her cell phone on the anchor desk before her. Then she looked at her watch. "I was told I would receive a call at 9:05 PM local time."

There was a long moment of silence. The tension in the studio was thick. No one said a word.

9:05 came and went.

Then 9:06.

Then 9:07...

I don't think Emma Steele liked being upstaged. There was a slight look of satisfaction on her face as the silence continued. "Maybe he lost your number?"

Reagan's eyes narrowed at her for a moment, then she brought her baby blues back to the camera lens.

The long-standing rule of television was that there should never be dead air. There should never be silence. That rule was getting broken.

"Maybe he got cold feet?" Emma said.

The phone rang a moment after that.

Reagan swiped the screen and put the call on speaker-phone. There was a microphone on the anchor desk nearby that picked up the caller's voice.

"Hello," Reagan said. "Who am I speaking with?"

A distorted voice filtered through the speaker phone. "The one you are all afraid of."

"Let me start this conversation off by urging you to turn yourself in. Enough harm has already been caused."

The killer laughed. "Where's the fun in that? They will have to catch me, if they can."

"So, this is a game to you?"

"Isn't everything a game?"

"You think ending someone's life is sport?"

"It is the greatest sport of all."

"Is that why you are doing this?"

"I could give you my reasons for doing this, but that would be boring. I don't ever want to be boring."

"I don't think anyone will ever accuse you of that," Reagan said. "You seem like an intelligent individual. You're methodical, calculating. Surely you have to realize the pain and suffering you are inflicting not only on your victims, but their loved ones?"

"Pain and suffering existed long before I came along."

"But you don't have to contribute to it."

"There is no pleasure without pain. No light without dark. No good without evil."

"Spare me the fortune cookie philosophy."

The voice chuckled. "I like this tough, sassy side of you. Carrying the torch for journalistic integrity. There's so little of that these days."

"What are you hoping to get out of all this?"

"What are *you* hoping to get?"

"You behind bars."

The killer laughed. "Give it your best shot."

The line went dead.

There was a momentary pause, then Emma Steele took over. "Well, that was riveting! Stay tuned. We'll be back after the commercial break with an expert panel of analysts to dissect every word of that conversation."

Emma smiled for the camera.

Reagan looked unsettled, then forced a smile.

"And, we're out to commercial," the production manager shouted.

Reagan pushed away from the anchor desk, took off her microphone that was pinned to her blouse, and set the wireless unit on the desk. She strode across the stage toward me as production assistants scampered about.

She didn't look happy.

"I'm not sure if that was a good idea, or a bad idea," Reagan said as she stepped to me.

I shrugged. "We can take the recording of the call and analyze the background noise. Maybe we can hear something that might giveaway the killer's location."

"I think all I did was give that asshole a platform."

"I think you made the right decision," I said. "Maybe somebody will recognize his speech pattern? Maybe we'll get a lead from the sketch?"

She looked at me curiously. "Since when are you on my side?"

"Just offering words of encouragement."

"You just want to get into my pants," she said, dryly.

"My encouragement was genuine and unmotivated by any personal desires."

She arched a skeptical eyebrow at me. "Well, buy me a drink, and play your cards right, and you just might get lucky."

21

Reagan's cell phone had been blowing up from the minute she stepped away from the anchor desk. It incessantly dinged with texts and social media notifications. She put her phone on silent and ignored it.

I could hear the damn thing buzzing in her purse, vibrating the table.

"To catching that son-of-a-bitch," Reagan said, making a toast.

“Here, here,” I said.

We clinked glasses, and I sipped the smooth whiskey.

We sat at a high-top table at *Beach Bums.* It was a party bar with an assortment of beer, liquor, and fruity drinks. Murals of the beach and crashing waves were painted on the walls. They usually had a *Best Bum* competition on the weekends, where one lucky lady was awarded a grand prize for having the fairest fanny.

The strip was relatively calm tonight. I'm not sure if it was just a slow evening, or if the shadow of the *Sandcastle Killer* was darkening people's enthusiasm for nightlife.

I scanned the crowd, then looked for security cameras. There were none. This was just the type of place that our killer liked to hunt—pretty girls, and a relaxed atmosphere.

"He's working the strip," I said.

"What can you do?" Reagan asked. "Can you stake the place out?"

"Sheriff Daniels has already doubled the patrols in this area. There's way too many bars to keep an eye on, and too much activity to follow."

"You don't have much else to go on right now."

"I know." I thought for a moment. "He's getting more cautious. He had taken pretty big risks dumping the first two bodies. This one would have been easy. Pull up to the reef in the middle of the night, toss the body over the gunwale, and slip away into the darkness."

"At least you know he's got a boat," Reagan said.

"Or access to one."

"Maybe you can cross reference registered boat owners with a list of violent offenders?"

"That's not a bad idea. But I have a feeling our guy doesn't have a criminal record. And I don't think this is the first time he's done this. He's too confident. Too slick."

"Can you look at a broader database, see if there are other killings with the same MO?"

"You're just full of good ideas tonight, aren't you?"

Reagan smiled. "I've been known to have them on occasion."

Her phone kept buzzing, and curiosity got the best of her. She reached into her purse.

"I wouldn't do that if I were you," I said.

"I know." She hesitated, then decided against it. "You're right, I'm just going to let everything go. I don't even want to know what they're saying about me on social media."

Reagan smiled at me, and her blue eyes sparkled. "I've been so stressed out. I just want to have a little fun. Is that too much to ask?"

"Hey, aren't you that reporter girl?" a girl asked as she passed by the table and recognized Reagan.

Reagan tried to hide a cringe. She put on a bright smile. "Yes, I am."

"I think it's absolutely disgusting what you did!"

Reagan's brow lifted.

"Don't you understand you're giving him exactly what he wants? That loser just wants to be famous. And you're helping him do that."

"I'm not helping him do anything."

"You're as monstrous as he is," the girl said, sneering at Reagan. "And you look fat on TV."

Reagan's face crinkled with shock.

The girl spun around and sauntered away.

“Can you believe that?” Reagan asked in disbelief.

“People have lost all manners.”

"I expected the interview to be controversial, but... What do you say we get out of here before someone else decides to give me an earful?” Then she added with a flirty glint in her eyes, “Maybe we can pick up where we left off last night?"

She didn't have to ask me twice. "I'll pay the tab."

I flagged down the waitress and gave her a wad of cash. Then I escorted Reagan out of the bar and we strolled down the sidewalk to her car. I helped her inside and told her I would meet her back at the boat. I had parked my bike a block away.

Reagan pulled away from the curb, and I strolled down the sidewalk to my X6. I pulled on my gloves and my helmet, then cranked up the beast. The roar of the engine echoed off the buildings on the strip as I let out the clutch and darted into traffic.

My mind filled with lustful thoughts, and my heart beat with anticipation. I was back at the marina in no time, hoping there wouldn't be any interruptions.

22

Reagan just couldn't resist. By the time I made it back to the *Wild Tide,* and stepped into the salon, Reagan's head was buried in her cell phone.

"You are not going to believe this!"

"At this point, nothing would surprise me," I said.

"My follower count is going up, and I have thousands and thousands of messages. They just keep coming. My phone is going off nonstop. Here, listen to this. These are some of the comments:

"You're so pretty.

"You're so brave, I hope you catch the killer.

"You're just another ho looking for fame.

"I've flushed things that were better looking than you.

"You automatically assume the killer is a man. He could have easily been a woman. You're so sexist.

"Watching the show gave me hemorrhoids."

I took the phone out of her hand, shut it off, and placed it on the settee beside her. I stared deep into her blue eyes. "No more phones. No more Internet. No more *Sandcastle Killer.* At least for the next hour."

A sultry glimmer flickered in her eyes. "You better last longer than an hour."

She leaned in, and our lips were on a collision course. We collided with an explosion of passion. And I finally got to taste those sweet, full lips that I had been lusting after.

I pulled her from the settee, placed my hand on the small of her back, and pulled her body against mine. My hands traced the delicate curves of her luscious form. Our hips mashed together, and I grabbed bountiful handfuls of her pert assets.

Buddy watched curiously.

I tried to get him to go below deck, but he wasn't listening, and I was far too distracted to really care.

Reagan's warm body felt like heaven. Our tongues danced, and our bodies melted into one another. I don't think we made it out of the salon until round two. The boat rocked, and moans of ecstasy filtered across the marina. Needless to say, Reagan got her full two hours worth—and then some.

We finally made our way below deck, and when we had worn ourselves out, I collapsed beside her in my bunk, a sweaty mess.

With my arm around her, she curled up next to me and stroked my chest.

"You're pretty good at that," Reagan said.

"Everybody has a gift," I said with a cocky grin.

She laughed. "I think, maybe, we should have done that sooner."

"You think?"

"We should probably do it again sometime soon," she said with a devious grin. "Just to make sure it wasn't a fluke."

"That can be arranged."

My whole body felt warm and tingly. I had forgotten about all the drama, all the killings, all the death and torment. The moment was pure bliss. I fell asleep with Reagan in my arms, and I slept like a baby.

I woke the next morning with rays of sunlight beaming through the portholes and the smell of bacon and fresh coffee in the air.

I crawled out of bed and staggered up to the salon.

"Morning, sunshine," Reagan said with a delightful sparkle in her eyes.

"Look at you being all domestic."

"I'm a lot nicer of a person when I get laid."

I chuckled. "I'll make sure you're in a good mood all the time."

Reagan pampered me and served me breakfast. She wasn't usually like this, and it caught me off guard. She sat across the table from me with a glowing smile. Her skin looked radiant. "See, I can be kind and caring at times."

"I see that."

Reagan was a passionate woman. When you were in her good graces, she clearly treated you like a king. But get on her bad side, and you'd feel her wrath. I was sure of that.

After breakfast, we decided to start the day off with a little exercise. We both worked up a healthy sweat, trying to break the mattress. We spent most of the morning frolicking in bed, and by 11 AM, it was time to stop fooling around and get on with the day. I climbed out of bed, took a shower, and put on some clothes.

Reagan slipped into the en suite after I was finished. While she was in the shower, Denise called.

"Hey, I have an idea."

"I'm listening."

"How about I create a fake profile on that website? I could set up dates with potential clients, and you and JD could be waiting in the wings ready to pounce. Maybe we can lure this guy out?"

My face crinkled. "Are you sure you want to do this?"

"Yeah. I mean, I don't *want* to do this, but I think it's necessary."

"I really don't want to put you in that kind of situation again," I said.

"I don't care what you want. It's not your choice."

My brow lifted, surprised. "Well, aren't you sassy?"

"As much as last time was uncomfortable, in the end, it did

some good. I don't want to see anymore girls killed in Coconut Key. I feel obligated to do everything I can."

I paused for a moment. "Okay. Let's do it."

"I already have all the sexy pictures from last time." Then she asked shyly, "Do you still have those on your phone?"

I stammered. "Strictly for law enforcement purposes."

"Yeah, right! Perv!"

"I'll text you a few to use for your profile images."

"Great! I'll let you know when everything is set up."

I hung up the phone just as Reagan stepped out of the en suite. She had a towel wrapped around her torso, and another towel twisted around her hair. The water beaded on her smooth shoulders. Damn, she looked good. I wanted to rip the towel off and get dirty again, but I figured I should actually get something accomplished today.

"Who was that?" Reagan asked.

"Denise," I said, hesitantly.

Reagan tried to pretend she wasn't jealous. "Who's Denise?"

She tried to make the question sound casual. Too casual.

"You know Denise."

"Oh, the hot redhead at the department?"

"I don't know if I'd call her hot."

Reagan rolled her eyes. "Please. I'm straight, and I'd fuck that girl."

A lightbulb of possibilities flashed in my mind. "That could be arranged, I'm sure."

Reagan's eyes narrowed at me. "I was kidding."

"Right," I said, trying not to envision a threesome.

Reagan moved close. "I know you've had more ass than a toilet seat, so I'm not going to get too possessive over you." She gave me a quick kiss. "Besides, I know you'll want more of this."

She smiled, stood tall, spun around, and dropped the towel as she stepped into the hallway, giving me a glimpse of her firm backside. It was a little teaser to keep me on the string.

She had me hook, line, and sinker.

Reagan got dressed and sauntered back to my room with her head buried in her phone again. It was the first time she had turned it on since I powered it off last night. She stared at the display with wide eyes. "I'm trending on social media. I've got a dozen messages from Harold. I've got to get down to the station. I guess I'll see you this evening?"

I smiled. "I guess so."

She marched up the stairs, and her high heels clacked against the deck.

I was already looking forward to her return.

23

"Oh, my God," Denise said. "I've had this profile up for less than two hours, and I already have 73 requests for a *date*."

"That's good," I said.

I had gone to the department to discuss our plan. Deputies buzzed about, desk jockeys did paperwork, patrol units brought in perps for processing. Phones rang, keyboards clacked, and the coffee machine percolated on the counter.

"It's creepy. That's what it is. One of the guys that wants to hook up is a friend of my dad's."

"I thought you used a fake name?"

"I did. I guess he saw my picture and messaged me. Who knows how long he's been using the site. Ew!"

"Is he rich?" I asked, teasingly.

She smacked me in the arm. "He's married. I know his wife. I've known him since I was a kid. It's weird."

"Are you going to tell your dad?"

"I don't know. If I did, I'd have to explain what I was doing on a prostitution site in the first place, and I don't think he needs to know that. He doesn't like me doing this job as it is."

We hovered over her computer terminal, perusing the possible *suitors*.

"Look for someone who resembles the sketch," I said.

"I don't think that sketch is very accurate."

"Me neither. But it's the best we've got to go on."

"What the hell are you two doing?" Daniels grumbled from across the room. He strolled to Denise's desk with a disapproving glare on his face.

I explained our sting operation to him. He paused for a long moment as he contemplated the situation. He scratched his chin. "I like it. Go with it. Way to take initiative, Denise."

He strolled away without saying another word.

Denise and I exchanged a surprised glance. It was usually never that easy with Daniels.

"Let's narrow this list down. We're looking for a white male, early 30s. For giggles, cross reference possible matches against registered boat owners."

"Aye-aye, sir," Denise said, mockingly.

The private messages kept flooding into her inbox. Some were nice and sweet, and the guys talked about how they wanted to love and take care of her and shower her with cuddles. Other messages were dirty and raunchy, describing proposed sexual acts in graphic detail. There were a number of messages that didn't say anything at all, and just included a picture of the applicant's *equipment*. She received pictures of everything from jumbo frankfurters to small breakfast sausages, and everything in between. Some were fresh out of the package, and some looked liked battle-scarred veterans of the sexual revolution. It was a horrific sight, and something I could have done without seeing. After the first one flashed on the screen, I said, "I'm gonna let you handle this. This really isn't my area."

Denise scowled at me playfully. "Great. Let me deal with this all by myself."

"Perks of the job," I said.

I pushed away from the desk and strolled through the station. I called JD to see how he was doing and I filled him in on the plan.

"So, let me get this straight. We're just going to go to a bar and watch Denise meet with prospective *Johns* she met online?"

"Yeah, pretty much."

"And do what? Wait till one of them tries to abduct her in an alleyway, or stuff her into the trunk of a car?"

"Something like that."

"And she agreed to this?" JD asked in disbelief.

"It was her idea."

"Really?"

"Really."

"Damn, I'm impressed."

"Let's just make sure nothing happens to her. Do you think you're up for this?"

"I feel great!" JD assured. "There's nothing wrong with me. You heard the doctor."

"If you say so."

"I'm *saying* so."

"Fine."

"Geez, what are you? My mother?"

"Just looking out for my friend."

"So, when is this going down?" JD asked.

"At the rate things are going, I think we could probably set up a few dates tonight?"

"Woohoo, it's party time!"

"The killer just disposed of one body. I guarantee he's out on the prowl for another. Hopefully we'll get lucky."

24

I had an uneasy feeling about the whole thing. But there was no turning back now. We took every precaution.

Denise sat at a high-top table not far from us. Small, flesh-toned earbuds allowed us to communicate with one another.

JD and I waited in the wings a few tables over, pretending to be inebriated and having a good time. We had decided to set *Beach Bums* as the meeting location. From what I could tell, it was a place the killer hadn't used yet to acquire a victim, but it fit his criteria.

Denise was all dolled up, wearing a skintight pair of hot pants and a bikini top. The outfit left nothing to the imagination. All of her glorious curves were on full display. Her flat, toned abs were a thing of beauty. She look cute and innocent and diabolically sexy at the same time. She was the girl next-door that could be naughty as hell. Every man's fantasy. The sultry red head was like a seal to a shark—and, hopefully, with blood in the water, we'd stir up a feeding frenzy.

"Radio check, over," I said.

Denise lifted her beer and took a sip, then whispered, "Copy that." Her voice crackled in my earbud.

I looked at my watch—it was 7:05 PM. The crowd was pretty thin at this point. The night was young, and you could still hear yourself think. The music got turned up louder and louder as the night went on.

"Your first date is late," I said.

"I'm aware of that."

"How far out did you space them?"

"Every half hour."

"Should have done every 20 minutes," JD said. "We'll be here all night."

"Well, next time, you can create a profile and meet with these creeps as often as you like."

JD frowned. "No, thanks. I'll leave that up to you."

A man in a suit stepped into the bar and glanced around. He was mid 40s and looked out of place. Everyone else in here wore shorts, jeans, T-shirts, bikinis, etc.

The man recognized Denise from her online images and took a seat across from her at the table. "Are you Melody?"

"I am," Denise said, extending her hand.

The two shook.

"I'm Alexander."

"It's nice to meet you, Alexander." Denise smiled. "Can I get you a drink?"

"Um, yeah, sure."

"What would you like?"

"I'll have what you're having."

Denise flagged the waitress down and ordered a beer for the man. The waitress was in on our sting operation. Her mission was to collect the bottle after Alexander had touched it. We could use it to match fingerprints and possibly DNA.

The waitress hurried to the bar and returned a few moments later with a cold brew. She used a napkin to set it on the table. We had already gotten a set of her fingerprints to rule out potential matches.

"Your profile says you're 32," Denise said with a healthy dose of skepticism.

"36," Alexander said, then smiled. "So I fibbed a little?"

He was still fibbing.

"That's okay," Denise said. "You don't look a day over 30." Now she was the one who was lying.

Alexander puffed up, basking in the compliment. "So, I've never really done this before," Alexander said. "How does this work?"

That was a fib too.

Denise smiled. "Well, we're just having a meeting to get to know each other and see if we might like to make some kind of *arrangement*."

"And what kind of arrangement would that be?"

"A handsome man such as yourself deserves the company of a good woman, does he not?"

Alexander smiled. "He does indeed."

"I'm great company," Denise said with a sultry grin. Then she made a pouty face. "Unfortunately, the cost of living is so high, I can barely pay my rent, my credit card bills, my car note..."

"And you need someone to take care of those for you?"

"Exactly."

"What kind of car do you drive?"

"A BMW convertible."

"That's a nice car."

"I like it."

"If I were to pay for your car note, what would that get me?"

Denise smiled. "That would get you dinner, drinks, and a little cuddle time. Once a month."

"What if I want to do a little more than cuddle?"

"Couples usually cuddle after they're intimate."

"So we'd have sex?"

"That's hitting the nail straight on the head, now isn't it?"

"I work hard for my money. I want to know exactly what I'm getting for that."

"I'm not a prostitute," Denise said.

A smug chuckle escaped his lips. "Of course you're not."

"If we decide to make an arrangement, I can guarantee you will be more than satisfied."

Alexander grabbed the bottle and took a sip of the beer. "And what, exactly, am I allowed to do to you?"

"What do you *want* to do to me?" Denise said, smoldering.

She was good at this. Denise played him like a fiddle.

It was easy to see that Alexander's hormones were surging. He tugged at the collar around his neck, and sweat misted on his forehead. He suggested a few places where he'd like to place his *weapon*.

Denise pretended to ponder his offer for a moment. "You can have access to door number one and two, if you pay for my car note. If you want access to door number three, you'd have to pay my rent *and* my note."

Alexander could barely contain himself. "You drive a hard bargain. But I might be able to swing that."

"I'll keep that in mind. It was a pleasure meeting you, Alexander," Denise said, subtly hinting that his time was over.

"What happens now?"

"I think about it, and I'll get in touch with you if I want to proceed."

Alexander deflated. "What's there to think about?"

Denise smiled. "Don't worry, Alexander. You want me to be choosy. So, when I choose you, you'll know my heart is in it."

A small smile tugged on Alexander's lips. "Okay, then. I guess I'll hear from you later?"

Denise nodded.

Alexander took his beer and pushed away from the table. He sauntered through the crowd toward the exit.

Denise whispered, "He's walking away with the bottle."

"I know," I said.

I flagged the waitress down and motioned toward the man as he strolled toward the door.

She ran behind him and snatched the bottle from his hand before he stepped onto the sidewalk. "I'm sorry, sir. You can't leave with the bottle."

His face crinkled, but he released the evidence.

The waitress darted back to the bar and placed the bottle in an evidence bag.

"We've got enough to bust that guy on soliciting prostitution," JD said. "Should we take him down?"

I thought about it for a moment. "I don't think he's our guy. Let's not waste the time. We'll get his prints off the bottle, and we can always bring him in later."

We recorded the whole thing with a small camera hidden among the condiments on Denise's table. She also had a small wireless camera in the necklace she wore.

The meeting with Alexander took roughly 15 minutes. We were still ahead of schedule.

Denise's second date was nothing like the first and didn't go as expected.

25

The guy limped to the table and politely asked, "Are you Melody?"

"I am," Denise said with a bright smile.

He shook her hand and said, "I'm Hunter."

He took a seat across from her at the high-top table.

Hunter was barely 27 years old. He was a skinny guy, shaggy brown hair, brown eyes, and had a soft-spoken demeanor. He was a mildly attractive guy, and probably could have done well without having to pay for it.

He glanced around, nervously.

"Is this your first time?" Denise asked.

"I'm kind of socially awkward, you could say."

"Me too," Denise said.

Hunter chuckled. "I don't believe that."

"No, really. I don't like big crowds. I'm not much of a partier. I like to curl up with a good book, or watch a scary movie."

Hunter smiled. "Me too."

He seemed relieved.

"So, what exactly are you looking for?" Denise asked.

"Um, well, you know..." Hunter stammered. "I'm just totally over the dating scene. I don't want to do it anymore. I'd just like to be able to spend time with somebody I enjoy. It's not about the sex, or anything like that. I just want to be with someone who I can be myself around and isn't going to lie to me or start unnecessary drama."

"I totally understand. I am so over unnecessary drama. You have no idea."

"I figure, if I'm paying you to hang out with me, then I know what I'm getting into. I don't have to worry about you running around on me because *that's* your job. I know that going into this."

"So you want a *girlfriend experience,* without the hassle?"

"Exactly."

"What happened, did someone break your heart?"

Hunter slumped, looking like a sad, pathetic puppy. "I blew out my ACL playing basketball. My girlfriend dumped me. Can you believe that shit? Just bailed when I needed her most. I guess I began to interfere with her social life? Kind of hard to go on adventures with a bum knee."

Denise made a sad face. "That's not cool. But it's her loss. You're so much better off now."

"I know," he said with his head hung low.

"I bet you're pretty mad at her?" Denise said.

"Oh, I was furious. I was so pissed off. I had stuck by *her* through all her bullshit."

"How long were you two together?"

"Six years. Six years, and she bailed on me like that." He snapped his fingers.

JD and I watched and listened to the conversation.

"This one's got a lot of pent-up aggression," JD muttered in my ear. "Maybe he's taking his rage out on these unsuspecting girls?"

"Could be," I said.

Denise continued, "Can I buy you a drink?"

"Yeah, sure."

"What would you like?"

"Whatever you're drinking is fine."

Once again, Denise flagged down the waitress. She held up her beer bottle and motioned to it, then signaled for two.

The waitress hurried over with two more beers. It was the best service anyone had ever gotten in a bar. That, in and of itself, should have been suspicious. But these gentlemen were too preoccupied with Denise to think about anything else. And who could blame them? She could make a dead man walk.

Hunter sipped his beer, then gasped with satisfaction. "So, how does this work?"

Denise gave him the sales pitch, and the price-list.

"Oh, okay," Hunter said, disappointedly, then slumped again. "So, the car payment is a little out of my budget range. I might be able to do that like every other month. Would that be cool? Like I said, I don’t need the sex part."

"We don't have to talk specifics now. We can work something out later."

"So does that mean that you want to see me?"

"I like to take my time with all new potential *friends*. So, I'll let you know." Denise smiled.

Hunter slumped again. "That means *no*, doesn't it?"

"No, it means I'll think about it."

It was like a switch had flipped. Hunter’s calm, pleasant demeanor vanished, and a rage-filled demon possessed him. His face snarled, and he growled, "You fucking bitch. You're just like all the rest of them!"

Denise's eyes went wide, and she leaned back, terrified.

Hunter glared at her for a moment, then pushed away from the table and stormed to the exit.

He left his beer bottle on the table, and the waitress snatched it up.

JD raised his eyebrows, and we exchanged a curious glance. "Seems like he might have some anger management issues."

Denise's voice crackled in my ear. "Did you get all that?"

"I did."

The waitress took a few steps, then the bottle slipped from her fingers and shattered into a gazillion pieces on the concrete floor. She gasped, and her eyes went wide, looking mortified. She glanced at me and flashed a sheepish shrug.

I shrugged back. Oh well. Trying to pull a fingerprint from the shattered remains would be a nightmare.

"Man, that guy got scary," Denise said. "The devil was in his eyes."

"Think he's capable of murder?" I asked.

"With a temper like that? I'd say he's a definite suspect," Denise said.

"Do you want to pick him up now?" JD asked.

"We don't have anything on him. He didn't solicit prostitution. He just wanted to *cuddle*, remember?"

"I'm going to follow him. See if I can get a license plate number or something. Can you handle things here by yourself?"

I nodded.

JD dashed out of the bar and went looking for Hunter.

Denise watched Jack leave, and concern filled her eyes. "Where is he going?"

"He's just going to tail the suspect for a bit."

"You guys are my backup."

"I'm not going anywhere," I assured.

"I'd feel better if both of you were around," she said.

"What? Don't you think I'll be able to protect you?"

Her eyes narrowed at me.

It was too late to argue. Her next date showed up. This guy was a real piece of work.

26

Denise's eyes sparkled, and she sat up straight. "Ooh, this one's hot!"

The guy looked like he had stepped out of the pages of GQ. He had dark hair, chiseled features, and ice-blue eyes. He was dressed impeccably, wearing a *Zangari* jacket and slacks, a *Domino Baldini* shirt, and *Augusto Cino* leather lace-up shoes. The gold *Färber* watch on his wrist cost more than the waitress would make in a year. He had a brilliant smile and a square jaw.

"You must be Melody," he said as he strolled to the table.

"I am," Denise replied.

"I'm Declan."

The two shook hands.

He took a seat, and Denise offered him a drink.

"No thanks. I never drink and drive."

"How responsible of you," Denise said, pretending to be impressed. "How about a glass of water?"

A thin, almost annoyed smile curled his perfect lips. "No thanks. I'm fine."

"Indeed, you are."

"I bet you say that to all the boys."

Denise smiled, innocently.

"So, how long have you been doing this?" Declan asked.

Denise hesitated. "I... I just started, honestly."

"I can tell," Declan said.

"Really? How so?" Denise asked.

“You still have a sparkle in your eyes. The ones who have been doing this for a long time... their eyes look dull and lifeless. They look at you, and they smile, but they're not really seeing you."

The way he said it was kind of creepy.

Denise forced a smile. She raised her beer, toasting to her self, "Here's to never losing that sparkle."

Declan smiled. "You are even more bubbly than I imagined."

Denise flirted, and Declan seemed enamored with her.

"I'll just cut to the chase," Declan said. "Money is not an issue. My time, and getting what I want, is."

"I aim to please," Denise said.

"I have a very particular set of desires. I want to be sure we are on the same page."

"How particular?"

"I like to role-play."

"Role-play is fun."

"You can feel free to say *no*," Declan said." "It wont hurt my feelings. Best we get this out of the way up front."

"Neither one of us wants to waste our time."

"Are you okay with being tied up?"

"What did you have in mind?" Denise asked.

"Nothing too extreme. Maybe a little spanking. A little hair pulling."

Denise didn't object.

"How about choking? I mean, not until you pass out or anything. We'd have a safe word, of course. We would stop any time you said the word."

"If I felt comfortable with the person, that wouldn't be a problem."

"I like to live life on the edge, Melody. I like to find the limits. That's where all the fun is."

Denise forced another smile. "I agree."

"How are you with pain?"

"Depends on what kind of pain we are talking about?"

"I find a mixture of pleasure and pain can be exhilarating. The contrast heightens pleasure, don't you think?"

"So you want me to inflict pain on you?"

Declan chuckled. "No. I like to dispense pain. Again, I'm not talking about anything extreme."

“You mean, you wanna pinch my nipples and spank my ass?”

“Maybe something a little more *intense* than that.”

“You're not talking about drawing blood, or leaving permanent marks, are you?"

“No. Nothing like that.” Declan paused. "I have to ask, are you a police officer, or in any way affiliated with law enforcement?"

"Do I look like a cop?"

Declan looked her up and down. "I can't say that you do. But the gentleman a few tables over, pretending not to be interested in our conversation, does."

Denise swallowed hard. She glanced to me. Then dismissed the whole idea as preposterous. "Who, that guy?"

Declan was spooked. He pushed away from the table. "Nice to meet you, *Melody*."

His tone suggested that he didn't believe Melody was her name.

I gritted my teeth and grumbled under my breath as *Mr. Model* strolled out of the bar. We didn't have anything on him. No fingerprints, and the name he gave was probably fake. I couldn't chase after him and leave Denise alone.

Denise looked at me and shrugged. She had several more speed dates lined up. This was going to be a long evening.

"That guy was a real freak show," JD said, his voice crackling in my ear.

"You heard that?" I asked.

"Clear as a bell. Hunter is a no go. He climbed into a cab and took off. We'll have to run his first name and his prints against the database to see if we can get a hit."

"I have a sneaking suspicion we are going to come up with a lot of suspects tonight, but nothing solid," I said.

"Denise sure can bring the perverts out," JD said.

"It's because I hang around you two so much," Denise grumbled.

By 10 PM, we were all burned out. The bar was starting to get crowded, and it wasn't conducive to conversation. After the last suspect, the three of us left *Beach Bums* and headed over to *Tide Pool* for a change of scenery.

The bar had an indoor and outdoor pool. Skimpy bikinis clung to hard bodies. Sometimes they didn't cling at all and ended up floating in the water. The music was chill, and caustics reflecting from the water danced on the ceiling. The place smelled like chlorine and whiskey.

JD wanted to sit on the back patio and enjoy the view.

There was plenty of eye candy for Denise to enjoy as well. Muscled men with beach bodies and washboard abs. It felt like spring break, and the bar served beer, mixed drinks, piña colada's, and various flavors of daiquiris.

JD had a thing for the bartender, Harper, at the outside bar. She slung drinks from a tiki hut, and JD always tipped her well.

I made it a habit to stay away from the fruity drinks. It could lead to wicked hangovers from all the sugar. Beer would do fine as we decompressed from the evening's interviews. We reclined on lounge chairs by the pool and watched the festivities.

People frolicked in the water. Wet feet slapped against concrete as girls sauntered around the pool, mingling, sometimes falling in, sometimes getting pushed. It was hard to sit this close to the action and not get hit with an occasional spray of water.

"We got so goddamn many suspects, I'm not sure what we're going to do with them all," JD said.

"Who knew there were that many creepers out there?" Denise said, sipping her strawberry daiquiri.

"And there are dozens more we didn't get to tonight," I said. "I'm afraid we can't do that every day."

"I feel dirty." Denise shivered. "I need to take a shower."

"Let me know if you need a hand with that," Jack said.

Her eyes narrowed at him. "Honestly, I don't know how much more of that I can do. It's draining."

"At least you didn't have to sleep with any of them," JD said.

"Can you imagine?" Denise said, thoroughly repulsed.

"No," JD said.

"What am I going to do when these guys figure out who I really am and they start stalking me in real life?"

JD and I exchanged an uncertain glance. We didn't have an answer for that.

"I mean, what if I happen to see one of them out casually? Like, when I'm going to the grocery store, or if I'm at a bar?"

I started to feel guilty about letting her do this. "You have to maintain good situational awareness. I want you carrying a weapon wherever you go. I don't care if you're running out of the house for just five minutes. You need to be packing."

"Trust me, I always carry," Denise said.

"Better safe than sorry," I said.

She slumped for a moment and sighed. "I guess I'm going to have to tell my dad I'm doing undercover work. I mean, what if his friend says he saw me on this website? Then I'm going to have some explaining to do."

"I think your dad's friend would have some explaining to do if he said anything."

Denise had a horrifying thought. "What if my dad uses that site?"

JD and I exchanged another wary glance.

"Nevermind. I don't even want to go there," Denise said.

"I'm sure your dad is a fine, upstanding member of the community," I said, trying to reassure her.

"I know. That's what freaks me out. If this job has taught me anything, it's the people that are the most buttoned up that have the most shady shit going on."

"I thought we were coming here to decompress," JD said. "No more shop talk." Jack lifted his beer. "To clearing our minds."

We clinked glasses and echoed the sentiment.

JD leaned back and watched as slippery bodies bounced and jiggled.

I leaned over and ribbed him a little bit. "Are you sure this isn't going to be too much excitement for you? Can your heart handle it?"

His eyes narrowed at me. "I'll handle it, or die trying."

My phone buzzed in my pocket. I pulled out the device and looked at the screen. It was Reagan. I swiped the screen to answer it. "Hey, what's going on?"

"Nothing," she said. "I just wanted to hear your voice."

"Well, it's nice to hear your voice too."

That drew JD's curious eyes.

"I just wanted to see what time you thought you'd be home?" Reagan asked. "I'm here, all alone," she said in a breathy voice. "Naked."

"That sounds interesting."

"I thought, maybe, if you got home before too late, we might, you know, see if last night was a fluke?"

I grinned. "It was no fluke."

Both JD and Denise were on the edges of their seats. They leaned in, trying to listen to my conversation. I shooed them away.

"We're just wrapping up a special operation and doing a post-op debrief. I should be back before too long."

"Hurry home," Reagan said before she hung up the phone.

I slipped the device back into my pocket and prepared for the onslaught.

"And who was that?" Jack asked.

"Reagan. She gets a little freaked out when she's by herself. She was just wanting to know when she should expect me."

A wry grin curled on Jack's face. He could barely contain himself.

Denise pretended not to be jealous.

"Looks like you've got yourself a *what time are you coming home girl*?"

I vehemently protested. "I do not have a *what time are you coming home girl*."

"Excuse me? What did she just ask you?"

I held my tongue for a moment. Then muttered, "*What time are you coming home?*"

"Your Honor, I rest my case."

"It's not like that."

"Oh, really? What's it like?" Denise asked.

"Are you sleeping with her?" Jack asked.

I hesitated. "Define sleep?"

Denise rolled her eyes. "You've got a *girlfriend*."

"I do not have a girlfriend."

"You're sleeping with her," Denise said. "She's calling you to find out what time you're coming home. And she lives on your boat."

I shrugged, innocently. "It's not my boat."

"She sure as hell ain't *my* girlfriend," Jack said.

The two of them giggled at my expense.

"There has been no discussion of formal terms," I said.

"Give it time," Jack said.

I scowled at him.

"Hey, whatever floats your boat," Jack said. "Find happiness where you can."

There was a long moment of silence.

I knew the grilling wasn't over yet.

"Have you given any thought to what happens when this goes south?" JD asked. "I mean, first it was just a few days. That ended up being a few weeks. Now, she's a permanent resident. What are you going to do, kick her off the boat when you get bored?"

"How do you know I'm going to get bored?"

Jack scoffed. "I've known you for a long time. It's impossible for you to settle down."

"You're one to talk. You settled down six times."

"Temporary insanity."

"Six times?"

"I'm a slow learner."

“I'm just waiting for the right one," I said.

"Is she the right one?" Denise asked. "Or is she *Ms. Right Now?"*

"Hey, ease up guys... Putting the cart before the horse, don't you think?"

Denise and JD laughed again.

"It's so much fun watching you squirm," Denise said.

I took a deep breath, exhaled, and sipped my beer.

“Well, you're gonna have to tell your roommate to find someplace else to stay tomorrow. We've got a charter.”

“Really?”

“I put it on the calendar. You should have gotten a notif- ication."

I shrugged. “Maybe I missed it? What are we doing?"

“You'll see,” JD said with a grin.

I could only imagine what he had lined up for us.

“Do we really need to keep doing charters?” I asked.

"Well, you might be loaded from doing a movie deal, but some of us have kids to put through college.”

I rolled my eyes. “I know you've got a pile of cash some- where. Don't pretend to be broke."

JD scowled at me.

We sat there in silence for a moment, then my phone rang again. I pulled the phone from my pocket and looked at the screen. It was Reagan again.

Denise and JD giggled.

"You two shut up," I said before answering. "Hey, what's going on?" I asked Reagan.

"He called," she said, her voice trembling.

"Who?"

"Mr. Sandcastle. Who do you think?"

"When?"

"Just now!"

"I'll be right there."

27

The glass of whiskey shook as Reagan lifted it to her full lips. She sipped the amber liquid, set the glass on the counter, and poured herself another. She was self medicating in the salon of the *Wild Tide* when I arrived.

"What did he say?" I asked.

"Nothing I wanted to hear." She took another sip of whiskey. "He abducted another girl."

My jaw clenched tight, and my hands balled into fists. "Has he killed her already?"

"No. She's still alive."

"How do you know that?"

Reagan looked at me with hollow eyes. "Because I heard her voice. She was terrified. Crying and screaming." Her eyes welled with tears. They soon overflowed and streamed down her cheeks, streaking her mascara. "It was horrible. It was the most gut-wrenching thing I've ever heard."

She ran into my arms and squeezed me tight. In between jerking sobs, she said, "He tortured her while I was on the phone. I begged him not to harm her. To let her go. I think that only a egged him on. He's sick. Twisted. He's thoroughly enjoying this."

Reagan sniffled and wiped her eyes.

"Why did he call you?"

"I don't know. To brag? I'm sure he doesn't have anyone he can talk to about this."

"And now you're his new best friend."

"I feel like I've invited a monster into my life."

"You didn't invite him in."

"Maybe not, but I sure as hell didn't have to open the door."

"Did he say when he's going to kill her?"

"No. He likes to play with his food before he eats." Reagan shivered with disgust.

I pulled out my phone and called the sheriff's office. I spoke with Deputy Trammel. "Have you received any *missing persons reports* in the last 24 hours?"

I heard his fingers clack against the keyboard. A moment later, he said, "Nope. Why? What's up?"

"I think we've got another missing girl."

He groaned. "Better let the sheriff know."

I hung up, called Sheriff Daniels, and filled him in on the situation.

"And you're sure about this?" Daniels asked.

"Yeah."

"Son-of-a-bitch," he grumbled. "Do we know anything about the girl? Was Reagan able to get a name?"

"We're you able to get a name?" I asked Reagan.

"Her name is Heather."

"Are you sure?"

Reagan shrugged. "That's what he called her."

I relayed the information to the sheriff.

"And your people can't trace this call?" Daniels asked.

"I've tried."

"With all your fancy connections, you're telling me you can't figure out where that bastard is calling from?"

"My contact tells me he's using an anonymous connection, probably from a mobile burner phone, then routing through multiple proxy servers, bouncing all across the globe. There's no way to track it. And even if you could, I can guarantee you will never be able to match that number to a person," I said. "I mean, that's how I'd do it."

"Keep trying. Pull whatever favors you can." Daniels hung up.

I called Isabella and asked her once again for help.

"Look, I've tried," Isabella said. "This guy knows what he's doing. He's either extremely tech savvy, or he's had experience in signals intelligence and knows how to avoid detection."

I thought about what she said for a moment. It struck a chord with me. "So, this guy could be former military?"

"Could be. Could be special ops."

"Do you think you could come up with a list of all former special operator's and clandestine agents that fit the profile and may have a connection to Coconut Key?"

"You mean, besides yourself?"

"Yes," I said flatly. "Besides myself."

"I'll see what I can do."

I hung up the phone.

"We've got to find that girl before he kills her?" Reagan said.

I felt completely helpless. Somewhere out there was an innocent young girl going through the most horrific experience of her life. And there was nothing I could do about it.

28

I woke the next morning with Reagan's silky body draped across mine. I was getting used to this sort of thing.

I peeled open my eyes, yawned, and stretched.

"What time is it?" Reagan asked, her eyes still closed.

"Time to get the show rolling. We have a charter this morning."

"Aw, does that mean we don't have time for fun?"

"No time for love today," I said.

Reagan was headstrong and didn't take *no* for an answer. Her delicate fingertips traced their way down my rippled abs and grabbed hold of the throttle. My engine was already started, and she revved it up.

"Are you sure we don't have time?" she asked in a sultry voice.

Before I could answer, she had submerged below the covers and made a very persuasive oral argument.

"I *guess* we might have time, if we make it quick," I said.

We proceeded to rock the boat, and I'm sure it sent ripples through the entire marina.

Somehow we managed to finish up, shower, get dressed, and make ourselves presentable by the time JD arrived.

He wasn't alone either.

I had stepped into the cockpit to drink my coffee and take in the morning air when I saw Jack parading five gorgeous women down the dock—all dressed in short-shorts and bikini tops. There were blondes, brunettes, redheads—all with svelte, toned bodies.

Jack grinned from ear to ear.

A nice camera with a large lens hung from a strap on his shoulder, and he had a collapsible reflector in his hand that was silver on one side and white on the other.

It didn't take a rocket scientist to figure out what was going on.

There was another man with him, as well as a woman who rolled a case behind her. She must have been a make-up artist or a stylist.

"Ladies, gentlemen," JD said. "Welcome aboard the *Wild Tide.*"

He motioned for them to board the boat, and the entourage stepped into the cockpit.

"This is my first mate and camera assistant, Tyson Wild," Jack said.

I smiled and shook hands.

JD introduced everyone. "This is Tristan. He is the owner of *Coconut Cream Sunscreen.* He'll be our art director today. This is Misha, the make-up artist. And we have Holly, Chloe, Megan, Emily, and Quinn. Did I get that right?"

The girls nodded with bright smiles.

JD tapped his noggin with his index finger. "I still got it."

"This is a really nice boat," Tristan said.

Tristan was tall, pale, and had strawberry blonde short hair. His round face was dotted with light freckles. He wore all black, which was a bad choice for a day in the sun.

"Thank you," Jack replied. "We can shoot around the boat, and I have the perfect location for the beach shots."

"Excellent," Tristan replied.

Jack said, "Tristan wants to shoot a calendar to promote his sunscreen. These five lovely ladies will be doing two months each, and one group shot for Christmas."

"You're missing a month," I said.

They all looked at each other confused.

I spelled it out for them. "Five girls times two is ten, plus a group shot—that's eleven. There are twelve months in the year."

"Oh, yeah, right," JD said.

"I know what we'll do," Tristan said. "We'll post preliminary shots of the girls on the web and have a contest to see who will be *Miss Coconut Cream*, and that girl will get the extra month."

Tristan muttered in my ear, "I didn't really have the budget for 12 months."

I gave him an understanding nod.

I showed the girls into the salon and gave them a tour of the boat.

Buddy went crazy, bouncing up and down, barking at the girls. He melted their hearts instantly, and they all knelt down and petted him. The little Jack Russell loved the attention.

Who wouldn't?

Reagan gave me the side-eye as I paraded these gorgeous beauties around the *Wild Tide.*

"I guess I'll see you later, babe?" Reagan said, marking her territory.

"Yeah, we'll be back this evening," I said, then looked to JD for confirmation.

"Yeah, shouldn't take long." He tried to stifle a chuckle, knowing he had created drama.

Reagan slipped out of the salon and into the cockpit. I heard her high heels as she marched down the dock.

JD elbowed me in the ribs and said with a healthy dose of sarcasm, "She didn't look jealous at all."

I scowled at him playfully, then escorted the girls below

deck and showed them to a guest compartment. It had four bunks. "You can store your belongings here and change in this compartment."

"Thanks, Tyson," they said, almost in unison.

They gave me flirty glances.

"Do you have our wardrobe?" Holly asked.

"I'll check with the make-up artist," I said. "I'm sure someone does."

"Well, this is a calendar for sunscreen," Quinn said. "Maybe there is no wardrobe."

"I'm fine with that," Megan said, pulling the string of her bikini top.

The fabric went slack and fell away, exposing her buoyant breasts.

It caught me off guard. I swallowed hard, and I couldn't help but let my eyes linger for a moment.

The girls giggled.

It's like they were purposely fucking with me. Reagan had marked her territory, and these girls were plotting an invasion.

I excused myself and climbed the stairs to the salon. I pulled JD aside and muttered in his ear. "What the hell are you doing?"

"What does it look like?"

"Have you ever done this before?"

JD's face crinkled dismissively. "How hard can it be? You point the lens at what you want to photograph, and you press the button. The damn thing has auto focus, focus tracking, auto exposure... Hell, it can probably wipe your ass for you. Relax. This is going to be fun." He thought about it for a moment. "Well, now that you've got a girlfriend, it might not be quite as much fun for you."

My eyes narrowed at him.

29

We stayed in the marina while the make-up artist plied her craft. It was much easier to paint a woman's face when the boat wasn't rocking on the swells.

As soon as one girl was prepped and ready for camera, JD went into action, posing the models and clicking photographs. He basically did everything he had seen the previous photographer do the last time we had models on the boat for a photo shoot.

The girls strutted their stuff around the dock and at various locations on the boat. Skimpy fabric hugged tight curves, and the girls' radiant skin shimmered in the sunlight.

The models didn't need much coaching. They knew exactly how to move their bodies, and what angles were the most flattering. They arched their backs, pushed their chests out, and smoldered into the camera.

It was hard to tell if they were selling bikinis, sunscreen, hair products, lip-gloss, or make-up. It didn't really matter. The girls were eye-catching, and that was the point.

I had never seen JD so focused in his entire life. He was almost giddy with excitement.

When we had gathered enough shots around the dock, we disconnected shore power and water, cast off the lines, and JD took the helm. He idled the *Wild Tide* out of the marina and brought the boat on plane when we hit the open water. The engines rumbled, and the boat left a frothy white wake.

The wind whipped through the cockpit as I sat in the mezzanine. There was something so relaxing about getting out on the water. All the turmoil seemed to dissipate. Even if we were technically working, it was an escape from everything that was happening on Coconut Key.

We cruised for a little while, then JD cut the engines and let the boat drift.

JD took more pictures of the girls lounging on the fore-deck, wearing sunglasses, and slathered with oil. A bottle of *Coconut Cream Sunscreen* was always nearby.

JD took several photos of the girls putting lotion on each other's backs.

Jack could barely contain himself.

I felt like I was on the set of an adult movie. Any moment now, the bikinis could fly off, cheesy music would start, and a plumber would show up to fix a leaky pipe.

The boat rocked gently with the swells. I watched with amusement as JD pretended to be a photographer.

"You do a lot of these shoots?" Holly asked.

"Here and there," I said.

"This is a really good gig to get. Tristan is great, and I think the company is really going to take off. It could be good for all the girls. I'm sure if he likes the photos, he'll book you guys for more."

I tried not to cringe. I had no idea how these photos would turn out. They could all be blank frames. At least, shooting digitally, I didn't have to worry about JD forgetting to put film in the camera.

"What about you? Do you model full-time?"

"Yeah. I do a lot of stuff for bikini brands and car magazines —hot rods, motorcycles, that kind of stuff. I've got my social media, and I'm building my follower count. I don't make huge money just yet, but I will," she said with a smile.

Jack took turns photographing the models around the boat, sometimes displaying the bottle of lotion. When he'd had his fill, he got behind the helm, cranked up the engines, and throttled up. He banked around and made for Angelfish Key Island.

There was a pristine secluded beach in a small cove. We'd taken photography clients there before. It didn't really matter where we took these girls. They were stunning, and it was almost impossible to take a bad picture.

Like Jack said, the camera did most of the work. Point, focus, shoot. A trained monkey could do it. Jack showed me some of the photographs on the camera display, and I had to admit, I was impressed. I had gone into this thing a little skeptical, but he *was* taking professional shots.

It took about an hour to get to Angelfish Key. We anchored

offshore and took the tender to the beach. The 7 foot inflatable boat had an electric outboard *Barracuda* motor that putted along at 5 to 7 knots. We had to make a few trips to get all the girls, gear, and make-up to shore.

I took Buddy with me on the last trip and sailed in on the surf. I hopped out of the boat and pulled the tender across the white sand to the tree line in the shade. I tied Buddy's leash to a tree branch to keep him from running off. I would take him for a run around the beach once we got situated.

This wasn't our first rodeo. JD and I had brought an ice chest with bottled water, soft drinks, and cold beer. We had a portable boombox, and some snacks, sandwiches, a few bananas, apples, and a handful of protein bars.

I asked the girls what kind of music they liked, and the general consensus was pop. I was an old school rock'n roll kind of guy, but I wasn't opposed to pop if it made the ladies smile.

Misha touched up the girls make-up, and before long, Jack was clicking away. He took photographs of the girls in the surf, and in the sand. Their hair blew with the breeze, and the sun glimmered on their skin. The make-up artist held the reflector, bouncing light into their eyes, making their skin look flawless.

It didn't take long for bikini tops to come off. The girls covered themselves with their hands, and for the most part, Jack kept the photos suitable for publication.

The girls slinked around in the sand, and granules clung to pert bottoms.

I think Jack found his second calling in life.

He gave me the camera and let me take a few snaps. I was pretty mechanically oriented, so it didn't take long to familiarize myself with the controls and start clicking away.

There are a few basic things to keep in mind with photography—the way light falls on your subject, the composition of your frame, and the energy of your model. Pointing your camera lens at pretty subjects and making sure they are in focus and well exposed is half the battle.

Not to brag, but my shots weren't too bad. I figured, with a little practice, I might be able to get good at this. Especially if we had girls *this* pretty to shoot all the time.

I got so involved in what I was doing, I didn't pay attention to what was happening out on the water.

A group of men in a *Go Fast* boat pulled alongside the *Wild Tide*.

Jack tapped me on the shoulder to get my attention and pointed. "Hey, look!"

I pulled my eye away from the viewfinder to see two men with their faces covered hop onboard the *Wild Tide* and dash into the salon.

I clenched my jaw and cursed under my breath.

30

Buddy barked incessantly at the thugs on the water.

I sprinted down the beach, grabbed the tender, dragged it into the surf, and hopped inside. I cranked up the electric motor and twisted the throttle. The tiny thing whined, propelling the boat forward. The bow launched into the air as it crested each swell. It wasn't the most powerful motor in the world, and fighting the surf was a challenge.

I raced toward the *Wild Tide* as fast as the tiny motor would go, hoping I'd get there before the thugs hot-wired the boat. The wind whipped through my hair, and salt water sprayed my face.

The driver of the *Go Fast* boat pulled a pistol and took aim. Muzzle flash flickered as he fired several shots in my direction.

The bullets snapped around me, splashing into the water. I ducked for cover and drew my pistol from my appendix carry.

With one hand on the throttle, and the other gripping my pistol, I fired back at the bastard.

He decided not to stick around. The engines rattled as he throttled up, and the *Go Fast* boat launched across the water, spitting a rooster tail of frothy water in its wake.

I was drawing closer to the *Wild Tide.*

The engines turned over, bubbling the water behind the swim platform. Just as I was getting close, the thugs throttled up, and the *Wild Tide* plowed forward.

I tried to keep up, but I was no match for the 40 knots the ship was capable of.

Before long, they vanished amid the swells.

A stream of obscenities flew from my mouth.

I took a deep breath, calmed myself down, and banked around, heading back to shore. I reached the beach moments later, then pulled the tender from the surf. I stomped across the sand with a scowl on my face.

"What just happened?" Holly asked.

"Somebody stole the boat," I said, dryly.

"Were those gunshots?" she asked.

I nodded.

"Holy shit! That's crazy."

"Does this mean we are stuck here?" Megan asked.

"No. I'll call the sheriff. Somebody will be here to pick us up soon."

I pulled out my phone and looked at the display screen. I was down to 15% of the battery. Worse, there was no cell service.

I grumbled to myself again, trying not to alarm the others.

"Is there a problem?" Megan asked.

"I can't get a signal."

"I left my phone on the boat," Tristan said.

"Me too," Megan added.

A chorus of people chimed in.

"I did too," Quinn said. "I didn't want to lose it in the water."

I glanced to JD. He was the only other person with a phone.

He checked the display. "No service either."

"I'll take the tender away from the island, maybe I can get a signal when I get out of this cove," I said.

I hopped back in the boat and fought my way out to sea. Once I had gotten out of the cove, I drifted with the current. I was a couple hundred yards offshore. Occasionally, a single bar of signal strength would appear on the display, then it would flicker off, back to *no service.* I tried a couple times to call the sheriff, but I was never able to connect.

I twisted the throttle, turned the boat around, and headed back to the beach. The little motor whined, then cut out as I entered the cove.

I closed my eyes and sighed, trying to remain calm. Everything was going wrong.

I used the oars to paddle to shore, gliding in on the surf.

The girls were starting to panic.

"We're you able to call for help?" Holly asked, her eyes wide.

"No, but we'll be okay. I'll hike up to the high ground and see if I can get a better signal there," I said. "I think we should set up camp before it gets dark."

"Camp?" Megan asked.

"In case we have to spend the night."

"Spend the night?" Holly said.

Their jaws dropped.

"Oh, no! No way. I'm not staying out here," Quinn said.

"Think of it as camping," I suggested. "We're in paradise. What could be better than a night under the stars? It won't be that bad."

"What about the bugs?" Megan asked.

"We'll build a fire," I said. "That will help keep them away. Plus, we packed some bug spray."

"We don't know what kind of animals are on this island?" Megan said.

"There's nothing to worry about," I assured. "Just a few tigers."

Her eyes rounded like saucers, and her face went pale. "Tigers?"

JD and I burst into laughter.

"I'm kidding. There are no tigers on this island."

JD and I gathered wood and brought it back to the beach and dug out a fire pit. Within a few minutes, we had a nice blaze going. The amber flames crackled high, and glowing embers floated on the breeze. We built a lean-to with fallen branches and large leaves. It wasn't much, but it would provide a little shelter.

Needless to say, the photo shoot was over. Our clients had gone into survival mode. Their flirty, sexy gazes turned into worried faces. Once we had camp set up, I headed into the forest to find high ground.

JD stayed with the girls and Tristan.

The sun dipped below the horizon, and the sky turned the purplish gray of dusk. There wasn't much elevation on this island, but I trekked up a hill that was maybe 40 to 50 feet above sea level. I climbed atop a tree and held my cell phone in the air.

Two bars of service.

Yay!

A confident grin curled on my lips. Then the notification flashed on my phone that I was below 5% battery.

I dialed Sheriff Daniels. It took a minute to connect to the network, then the phone rang a few times.

Just as Daniels answered, the call dropped.

I called again.

Dropped.

I dialed a third time, and the phone went dead.

My jaw tightened, and I wanted to throw the phone against a nearby rock.

Could anything else go wrong?"

I knew better than to ask.

31

I climbed down the tree, hiked back to the beach, and borrowed JD's cell phone. I made the trek back up to high ground, climbed the tree *again*, and attempted to dial the sheriff's number. Jack had a different service provider, and I couldn't get a signal.

Now I was starting to get concerned.

I didn't mind sleeping on the beach. That would be like a five star hotel compared to some places I'd had to bed down in the past. But I was concerned about our guests. They weren't used to this kind of thing. We had plenty of food and water to get us through the next 24 hours. But after that, things could get dicey.

There was enough vegetation on the island that I was sure we could sustain ourselves, but it wouldn't be pretty.

I figured when Reagan didn't hear from me, she'd either be worried sick, or mad as hell. Spending the night on a deserted island with five gorgeous bikini models would take a lot of explaining, no matter what the circumstances. *Even if she wasn't technically my girlfriend.*

We all huddled around the fire in silence—the amber glow flickering across our faces.

"What happens now?" Holly asked.

"We wait until someone comes by the island," Jack said.

"How long will that take?"

He shrugged. "I'm sure it won't take long."

"What about the inflatable?" Megan asked.

"The battery is dead," Jack said. "It's a long way to row back to Coconut Key."

"But that's an option, right?" Megan asked.

"It's 30 miles back to Coconut Key," JD said. "That's about 10 straight hours of rowing, in good conditions."

"I was planning on paddling out until I got a signal," I said.

"You're going to paddle out there at night?" Holly asked, concerned.

"It's no big deal."

"I'd be scared to death out there. What if you get lost?"

I chuckled. "I'm not going to get lost."

"The current could take you out to sea."

"Don't worry," Jack said. "Tyson is a professional."

"What's that supposed to mean?"

"We were both in the Navy. This wouldn't be the first time he's taken an inflatable boat out to sea at night."

Holly's eyes brightened in the fire light. She looked curious and excited. "Were you like, a Navy SEAL, or something?"

A slight grin curled on my lips. "Something like that."

A seductive glimmer filled her eyes. "So, how serious is this girlfriend of yours?"

She did an unconscious flip of the hair and arched her cleavage ever so slightly.

I chuckled, nervously, and headed to the tender without answering. She would be hard to resist.

I grabbed a bottle of water, a protein bar, and a flash light. Before dragging the boat into the surf, I said to JD, "Look after Buddy."

32

The fire on the beach was a speck on the horizon. My shoulders burned, and my chest heaved for breath as I rowed farther away.

I was definitely getting a workout in.

The tiny boat rose and fell with the swells. I kept checking every few minutes to see what the cell reception was like. The thought of having to row all the way back to *Coconut Key* filled me with dread. My arms would likely rip out of their sockets.

I took a breather, drifting along the inky water. The sky was pitch, and the blanket of clouds overhead blocked the moonlight. I pulled out JD's cell phone and got a single bar of service. I dialed the sheriff again.

This time he answered.

"I have a little bit of a situation," I said.

I explained to him that we were stuck on Angelfish Key.

"You mean to tell me you're actually complaining about being stranded on an island with five bikini models?"

"I don't know if I'd call it *complaining*, but we could use a rescue."

"Shit, being stranded like that sounds like a *rescue* to me. Want to trade places?"

I chuckled.

The sheriff said he would either come get us himself, or send another deputy. It would take him at least an hour to get here.

I hung up the phone and began rowing back to shore. In the distance, I saw the running lights of a boat on the horizon. I pulled out my tactical flashlight and signaled the passing vessel. It was a 65 foot yacht. I waited for a hopeful moment, but the boat kept on going.

I pulled the oars against the water, knowing I'd be sore as hell in the morning.

I reached the beach, and pulled the tender ashore. The girls were relieved when I informed them of our pending rescue.

Holly offered to give me a back massage to soothe my tight, sore muscles.

Who was I to decline?

I sat in the sand by the fire while she dug into my rotator cuff muscles. Her hands felt sublime.

"You know, if this modeling thing doesn't work out, you could do well as a massage therapist," I said.

She laughed. "Thank you."

"But I'm pretty sure the modeling thing is going to work out."

"I'm having fun with it."

"Hey, don't I get a massage?" JD said, feeling left out.

The girls gave him eye rolls.

"I've been lifting this heavy camera all day, making you all look gorgeous." He tried to draw sympathy with a pathetic face.

"Aw, poor baby," Quinn said. She mocked him like he was a toddler. "You had a really rough day, didn't you?"

"I did. It takes work to do justice to your true beauty." JD grinned.

I guess she felt sorry for him because she slid over and started squeezing his traps. A look of pure pleasure washed over Jack's face as she rubbed his neck and shoulders.

"Now that's what I'm talking about," JD said.

Since we were getting rescued, and didn't have to worry about dehydration, we got into the beer and decided to turn this into a beach party while we waited. The music bumped from the boombox, and we all enjoyed ice cold brews.

A little over an hour into our impromptu party, the sheriff's patrol boat rumbled across the water. The boat had a shallow enough draft to get into the cove. He shouted at us through a bullhorn as he pulled close to shore. "There's no overnight camping on this beach. You're all under arrest!"

He said it with a hard voice and stern face.

"Is he serious?" Megan asked.

I chuckled. "That's a rare example of humor from Sheriff Daniels."

We snuffed out the fire, gathered our belongings, and trudged into the surf, loading our gear aboard the patrol boat.

Jack and I helped the girls aboard. We transferred Buddy aboard, then we climbed in, along with Tristan.

"I never thought I'd be so excited to see a cop," Quinn said.

Sheriff Daniels gave her a sideways glance.

"Thanks for coming to get us," I said to the sheriff.

"You didn't have to get here so fast," JD muttered. "Another hour and I think I might've gotten somewhere."

"How is that you two always seem to get yourselves into these situations, yet still come out smelling like roses?" the sheriff asked.

"Charmed life," JD said with a wide smile.

"One day, that *charm's* going to run out," Daniels said.

"Talk to my ex-wife. She'll tell you my charm left a long time ago."

"Which ex-wife?" the sheriff quipped.

Daniels reversed away from shore, then banked the patrol boat around and throttled up the engines. We crashed through the surf, heading into the inky blackness.

"I got a call from the station on the way out here," Daniels shouted over the engines. "A deputy picked up a suspect you boys might want to take a look at."

"Really?" I said, curiously.

"Pulled him over on a traffic stop. The guy was acting nervous, so the deputy searched the vehicle. Found a gram of cocaine. Then searched the trunk and found a knife, rope, and duct tape. White male, early 30s. Fits the profile."

I exchanged an optimistic glance with Jack.

We raced through the night, back to Coconut Key. Jack took a seat next to Quinn and continued to work his magic. It looked like she was softening up to him a little.

Daniels dropped us off at the marina at *Diver Down.* We told him we'd meet him back at the station shortly. Once we had unloaded all of our gear, Daniels idled the patrol boat out of the marina.

"Well, that was an adventure," Tristan said.

"Sorry about all the excitement," JD said.

"Are you kidding me? I've got great photos for my calendar and an amazing story to tell about how we got them. This is going to launch the brand. It will go over great with adventure seekers." Tristan smiled. "Anyone into extreme, outdoor sports needs to look after their skin."

Holly gave me a hug and whispered in my ear. "You know how to find me on social media. Message me sometime. I'd love to finish that back rub."

She kissed my cheek and batted her eyelashes before spinning around and sauntering down the dock with the rest of the girls.

"What a day!" Jack said, admiring the view.

We stood on the dock next to the empty slip where the *Wild Tide* should have been. It was hard to believe the boat was gone.

Jack looked at the empty water and sighed. "I guess you don't have a live-in girlfriend anymore."

"I got no place to live. Think we'll get the boat back?" I asked.

JD frowned. "I give it 50-50."

We strolled down the dock and put what was left of our gear behind the bar in *Diver Down.* It was a little after 11 PM.

"What happened to you two?" Madison asked.

I told her the story.

"Reagan was in here earlier," Madison said. "I think she was starting to get annoyed."

"Circumstances beyond my control." I said. "Do you have Reagan's number in your cell phone?"

"Yeah," she said.

"My phone died, and I don't know her number by heart."

Madison handed me her phone, and I called Reagan.

"Hey, Maddy," Reagan said when she answered.

"It's me, Tyson."

"I tried calling earlier, but it went straight to voicemail. Did you have fun with the models?"

It was a loaded question.

"I think we got some really good pictures."

"Good for you," she said, flatly. I could tell she wasn’t thrilled. "I waited around at *Diver Down* for a while, then when you didn't come back, I decided to go back to my place."

There was more than a little attitude in her voice. But that changed when I said, "The boat got stolen."

"What?"

I filled her in on the details.

"That's insane. How did you get back to Coconut Key?"

"The sheriff picked us up. We just got back."

"Well, you can stay with me, if you need a place?"

"It's either that or Jack's couch."

"I can assure you, my bed is much more comfortable."

"I'm sure it is," I said.

“How’s Buddy?”

“He’s fine. But Fluffy was on the boat.”

“That makes me so mad!”

“You and me both. I’m worried about her.” I paused. "I've got to run down to the station. We have a potential suspect to interview. I don't know what time I'll finish up."

“Related to the boat or the killings?”

“Possibly the killings.”

"I’d leave the key under the mat for you, but I don't really feel comfortable doing that with a serial killer running around."

"I don't blame you. It could be late. I'll crash at JD's tonight and catch up with you in the morning."

She let out a disappointed sigh. "I guess I can live without you for one night."

I grinned. "I'll talk to you later."

I hung up and handed the phone back to Madison. “Can you look after Buddy?”

“Sure thing,” Madison said.

I knelt down and petted the little Jack Russell. “You be a good boy for Aunt Maddy.”

He barked.

“I never thought I'd hear you say you're worried about a cat," JD muttered, eavesdropping.

“Well, I better get her back unharmed, or those assholes are going to be in for a world of hurt.”

JD and I left *Diver Down* and headed to the station. When I saw the suspect sitting in the interrogation room, I was confident we had our man.

33

"So, you don't drink and drive," I said. "But you've got no problem with a little cocaine?"

"I don't know what you're talking about," Declan said.

He was one of Denise's dates from *Beach Bums*.

The suave playboy didn't look so suave now. I sat across the table from him in an interrogation room.

"What are you doing with the rope and the duct tape?"

"Is it illegal to travel with hardware supplies in your car?"

"You don't seem like a handyman to me."

"Oh, I come in pretty handy. Just ask the ladies." He smiled.

This guy had an overinflated view of himself.

"Where is your hospitality?" Declan asked. "Aren't you going to offer me a drink. Perhaps a snack?"

I wanted to smack the smug grin from his face. He sat in the chair with his hands cuffed behind him. I ignored his request.

"Where were you headed when you got pulled over?"

"I don't think that's any of your business."

"Right now, you're looking at felony possession of a controlled substance. I'd cooperate, if I were you?"

"Well, sadly for you, you're not me, and I want to talk to my lawyer."

That was it. Once he asked for an attorney, I could no longer question him.

I left the interrogation room and joined Sheriff Daniels and JD in the hall. "You think we have enough to get a warrant?"

"To search his house?" Daniels asked.

I nodded.

"On what grounds? Except for the coke, the items we found in his car aren't illegal. There is no indication that he is connected with the killings."

JD's face twisted. "Are you kidding me? The guy is a freak. We've got surveillance footage of him soliciting Denise for lewd and lascivious acts."

"I've seen the footage," Daniel said. "He never solicited her directly. He talked around it... but there was never an explicit offer of money for sex."

"He wanted to tie her up," JD protested. "He's got rope in the car. Put 2 and 2 together."

Daniels frowned. "Nothing wrong with a little rope-play between consenting adults."

"I don't think any of these bodies we've been finding consented," JD said.

"Is there anything to indicate that he used rope on his victims?" Daniels asked. "Have we recovered any rope fibers?"

JD glanced to me.

"No," I said. "It's likely he restrained his victims with either rope, zip ties, or with duct tape. But Brenda hasn't been able to pull anything conclusive."

"Declan's the best lead we've got," JD said. "He could have that missing girl held captive right now, tied up in the basement, waiting to be slaughtered."

Daniels sighed. "I'll see if I can get you two a warrant." He paused, then casually said, "You could always do a *knock and talk.* Who knows, you might find something that would give you reasonable suspicion to believe a crime is in progress?"

A sly grin curled on JD's lips. He elbowed me in the ribs as Sheriff Daniels strolled away.

Daniels wasn't telling us to break in to Declan's house, but he was suggesting we use our powers of creativity to find a way inside.

34

JD didn't even bother with pretenses. We strolled up the driveway to Declan's front door, and JD kicked it open without a second thought. The doorjamb splintered, and the large panes of glass in the door shattered. Shards, like tiny diamonds, bounced across the foyer.

The home was a two-story, with sleek lines, lots of glass, and open spaces. The backyard overlooked the beach. Declan certainly did well for himself. It reminded me of the kind of exotic home you'd see in the Hollywood Hills. A home that could be the set of a movie, or appear in *Architectural Digest.*

"I heard somebody scream," JD said with a wink. "Didn't you?"

I didn't hear shit.

With his pistol in the firing position, JD advanced into the home, glass crunching beneath the soles of his checkered *Vans.*

There was an alarm panel on the wall, not far from the door. Fortunately, it hadn't been set.

The lights were on in the living room. It was a large space with a high vaulted ceiling. Gray hardwood floors gave the place a clean, elegant feel. The floor-to-ceiling windows offered a view of the back patio, infinity pool, and the inky black ocean beyond. I could hear the waves crash against the shore.

"You know if we don't find anything, Daniels is gonna have our ass," I said.

"So we better find something!"

We swept through the living room and the kitchen, clearing the area with tactical precision—the barrels of our pistols panning from side to side.

There were large canvases of art on the walls. Mostly abstract. Statues sat atop pedestals. Declan was a collector and had a good eye.

We cleared the downstairs and didn't find anything of note. Then we pushed up the staircase and down the hall, toward the master bedroom.

We passed by a door that looked odd. It was in an interior hallway, but had a deadbolt that latched from the outside.

It was designed to keep someone locked in the room!

JD and I exchanged a curious glance.

He twisted the deadbolt, and it made a loud clunk.

A whimper filtered from the room.

"Did you hear that?" Jack asked.

This time, I really heard it. He wasn't bullshitting.

JD pushed open the door, and we flooded into the room.

A young girl was bound and gagged, her wrists and ankles tied to each corner of the four-post bed.

She was completely naked.

With a red ball gag in her mouth, her screams were muffled, but her eyes widened when she saw us, and her screams grew even louder.

JD flashed his badge, trying to calm the young woman.

It must have been a horrible sensation to be in such a compromised position with two strangers entering the room.

JD's shiny gold badge did little to sooth her anxiety.

I covered her with a blanket, then JD and I untied her bonds. The stunning blonde reached back and unlatched the ball gag once her hands were free. That's when her tirade began. "What the fuck are you doing?"

"Saving your ass from a sadistic man," JD said.

A scowl twisted on the woman's face. "What the fuck is your problem? Do you two dipshits have a warrant?"

JD and I exchanged a curious glance.

"Get the fuck out of here!"

"You're not here against your will?" I asked.

She glared at me. "No."

JD arched a surprised eyebrow. "Whoops. My bad."

"Where's Declan?" the girl asked.

"He's been arrested for possession of a controlled substance," I said.

She let out an exasperated sigh. "For fuck's sake. He told me he would just be gone for a moment."

"See, aren't you glad we came along?" Jack asked. "You could have been here for days."

She softened a bit, accepting the fact that a few days tied to the bed without food or water could be detrimental. "Did he tell you I was here?"

"No," JD said.

"So, he was just going to leave me here?" she asked, annoyed.

We shrugged.

"So, this was strictly consensual?" JD asked.

"Yes." She paused. "Would you mind giving me a little privacy while I get dressed?"

"Sure thing, ma'am," I said.

We stepped out of the room and waited for her in the hallway. A few moments later, she pulled the door open, dressed in a short skirt, high heels, and a cute top. "I'm not in any kind of trouble, am I?"

"Not at the moment," I said.

Her eyes narrowed at me "So, I can go, right?"

"I'd like to ask you a few questions first."

"Like what?"

"What's your relationship to Declan?"

"He ties me up and fucks me," she said, flatly. "I kind of like it." Her eyes shifted between the two of us. "And don't pretend you two haven't ever handcuffed a girl to a bed and did dirty shit to her."

Jack raised his hands innocently. "No judgment here."

"How did you meet Declan?" I asked.

"I'd rather not say."

"So, I take it this relationship you have with Declan involves a monetary exchange?"

Her cheeks flushed with rage. "Let's get one thing straight, I am not a hooker. I don't screw guys for money."

"Just for favors, right?" JD asked.

She glared at him again. "I'll have you know that I happen to like having sex with Declan. He's really good in bed, and he's got a big..." She stopped, then changed the subject. "Why are you guys asking these questions, anyway?"

"We thought he might be connected to the killings," I said.

Her eyes widened. "You mean, the *Sandcastle* thing?"

I nodded.

"Oh, my God, you don't think that's Declan, do you?"

I shrugged.

"No," she protested. "No way!"

"Why do you say that?" I asked.

"Because, he's had plenty of opportunities to kill me, and I'm still here."

"How often are you here?" I asked.

"She thought about it for a moment. "We have an arrangement. Maybe twice a week?"

"And what do you get in return?" JD asked.

Her eyes narrowed at him again. "Like I told you. I'm here because I want to be. I mean, it may have started as something else, initially, but I kind of like what we have. He's loaded, good looking, and helps me out when I need it. That's more than I can say for a lot of guys I've dated."

I asked her if she met Declan on the website, and she finally acknowledged that she did. "You're not going to bust me for, like, prostitution, are you? Because that's totally not what this is."

"We're not going to bust you," I said.

"So, you get compensated for what you do?" JD said.

She sighed. "So what? He buys me things. He pays for my rent. I get nice jewelry and nice clothes, and I don't have to worry about anything." A smug smile curled on her plump lips. "I'm just like a suburban housewife. Except that I don't cost nearly as much. Ex-wives can be expensive. Ex-playthings, not so much. Pay now, or pay later."

"Ain't that the truth," JD said.

"Has Declan ever become violent?" I asked.

A naughty glimmer flickered in her eyes. "Only when I want him to be."

"Do you know how many other women he sees?"

"We don't talk about that. He has his playthings, and I have my boy-toys. I know this whole thing could end tomorrow, so I'm getting what I want while I can."

"Have you ever noticed anything suspicious about his behavior?" I asked.

"I don't keep tabs on him. And no, he's never had blood-stains on his clothes or anything crazy like that." She folded her arms. "If you guys think Declan is the killer, you're barking up the wrong tree. He's never pushed me beyond my limits and always stops when I say our safe word."

It looked like our raid was a bust—and the county had a front door to pay for. I could only imagine the heat we were going to take on this one.

35

It was well after midnight by the time we got back to JD's. Scarlett was on the couch, watching TV. She wore fuzzy socks, and a long T-shirt. I'm not sure what, if anything, she had on underneath the shirt.

"You're going to have to vacate," Jack said to her. "Tyson is crashing on the couch tonight."

"Why? What happened?" Scarlett asked. "Did Reagan kick you out of the boat?"

She laughed.

I sneered at her. "No. It got stolen."

"What?" Her eyes widened.

We caught her up to speed on the details.

"That sucks," Scarlett said. "You can take my bed, and I'll crash on the couch."

"Thanks. The couch is fine."

"Are you sure? I've been sleeping out here most nights anyway, watching TV."

Scarlett was 18 and hell on wheels. She'd been trying to keep her nose clean ever since her arrest for possession. But she seemed to have a nose for trouble. I didn't trust her for a second.

"I appreciate the offer. I'll be fine on the couch."

Scarlett shrugged. "Suit yourself."

She pulled herself off the couch and said, "I'll get you some sheets and a pillow."

She scurried away and returned with the linens momentarily. She helped me make an impromptu bed on the couch.

"Did Jack tell you? I'm cleared to go to Los Angeles. I talked to Joel, and he wants me to come out as soon as possible. Jack said you might be able to take me out there and show me around?"

"I *might* be able to do that."

"And you better keep your ass out of trouble," JD said to her.

Scarlett squinted at him. "Relax, Jack. Have I gotten into any trouble lately?"

Jack didn't have a retort.

"I've been a good little girl. I go to work, I come home, I watch TV. I don't drink, I don't do drugs, and I'm not out running the streets."

I gave her a skeptical glance. I knew damn good and well she was smoking a little weed from time to time.

"If I even get an inkling of trouble from you while you're out there, I'll send Tyson out to yank your ass back so fast it'll make your head spin."

Scarlett rolled her eyes. "I'm an adult, Jack. Maybe you should start treating me like one?"

"Maybe you should start acting like one? There's a thought."

She rolled her eyes. "You screw up one time..."

Jack muttered, "It was more than one time."

"Enough, already," I said. "It's been a long day."

There was a long moment of silence in the room as the tension settled.

"I'm gonna hit the hay. I will see you people in the morning." Jack pointed at Scarlett. "Behave."

She rolled her eyes again.

Jack sauntered into his bedroom and closed the door.

"I swear to God, he's so uptight," Scarlett said.

"I can't imagine why?" I said, my voice dripping with sarcasm.

She smacked my arm playfully. "Don't take his side."

"I'm not taking sides."

She arched an eyebrow at me.

I raised my hands innocently.

"I was thinking, maybe we could go to Los Angeles next week?"

"I can't go anywhere until we wrap up this case."

Scarlett gasped. "You and I both know this thing could drag on forever. How many serial killers are out there running around that have never been caught?"

"Is that a rhetorical question? Because I can give you an answer. The FBI will tell you there are, on average, 50 at large. But some statisticians say there are 2000 active serial killers nationwide that are unaccounted for."

Her eyes widened. "Are you serious?"

"As a heart attack." It probably wasn't the best phrase to use, considering Jack's recent trip to the ER.

The shock wore off momentarily, and Scarlett refocused on her ambitions. "I'm sure you can break away for a day or two in Los Angeles. It's not going to kill you?"

"Have you ever been to Los Angeles?"

"No."

"The traffic alone is enough to kill a person."

She huffed and gave me a look that only a teenage girl could give. "Fine. I guess we'll just never know what could have happened with my career," she said in a dramatic fashion. "There are opportunities passing me by as we speak. But, I understand."

She gave me a sad, pouty face.

"The whole *guilt trip thing* is not going to work on me."

Scarlett smiled. "Yes it will. I can be very persuasive."

"I know."

"But my powers don't seem to be working on you at the moment. Why is that, Mr. Wild?"

She wasn't just talking about the trip to Los Angeles.

"There is a whole host of reasons."

She made a pouty face again, turning out her bottom lip. In a breathy voice she said, "Are you sure you don't want to sleep in my bed? It's super comfortable."

Her silken words slipped from her lips and lingered in the air.

“Go to bed, Scarlett,” I said, rolling my eyes. “I’m immune to your charms.”

She smirked. “It’s so fun to make you uncomfortable.”

Scarlett brushed past me and strutted toward her room, putting an extra sway in her hips. She peeled off her T-shirt along the way. With a devilish glance over her bare shoulder she said, “Immune, eh?”

36

It was a disaster waiting to happen.

I decided it was not a good idea to crash on Jack's couch. I snuck out and caught an Uber to the *Seven Seas.* It was far too late to go banging on Reagan's door.

I strolled into the posh lobby in the wee hours of the morning. There was no one at the front desk. I waited for a moment before someone came out from the back.

"Can I help you?" a woman asked.

"I'd like to rent a room."

"I'm sorry," the woman said, insincerely. "We are all booked up. There is a convention in town."

"You don't have *anything* available?"

"That's what all booked up means," she said with a forced smile.

I decided to play the law enforcement card and flashed my badge. "Are you sure?"

"I'm positive."

"Okay, thanks. You've been helpful."

I backed away from the check-in counter and strolled through the lobby. I took a seat on the couch not far from the baby grand piano. The check-in girl left the desk and went into the back room.

The lobby was empty.

The bar was closed.

The trickle from the waterfall echoed across the cavernous space. It was the only activity, at the moment.

I left the couch and strolled out to the pool. Underwater lights illuminated the clear water. I found a lounge chair in the corner and decided that would be as good a place as any to bed down for the rest of the night. I just needed to grab a few hours of shut eye.

I closed my eyes and nodded off. The next thing I knew, the sky had turned a pinkish gray color, and a large man in a suit jacket hovered over me. The sun would crest the horizon soon.

The man had a walkie-talkie in one hand and a gold acetate name tag above his left breast pocket. He was hotel security, and he was asking me, "Excuse me, sir. Are you a guest of the hotel?"

I squinted at him through sticky eyes. I fumbled for my badge and flashed the shiny gold thing. "I'm deep undercover."

He chuckled. "What's the matter, deputy? Did the wife kick you out?"

"No. I'm a liveaboard, and my boat got stolen."

"No shit?"

I told him the story.

"Damn, that sounds like it was a nice boat. And you can afford that on a cop's salary?"

"Long story. It's my buddy's boat. He lets me stay there. It pays to have friends who invested well."

"I was about to say... If you can make that kind of money as a deputy in this town, I'm in the wrong business."

I chuckled.

I guess he took pity on me, because he said, "Come with me. I've got a place you can stay for a few hours. I just can't have you sleeping poolside, looking like a vagrant."

I pulled myself off the lounge chair and followed the man to a spare room. He slipped his master key into the slot, and a light flashed green on the card reader. He pushed open the door and flicked on the lights. "We always keep a few rooms empty in case of emergency. Mostly for staff use. You can stay here till noon."

I was stunned by his generosity. "Thank you. That's very kind."

"Just remember, I did you a favor. If I ever get in trouble with the law..." He smiled.

I grinned back at the man.

"If anybody gives you any trouble, tell them Big Carl said you could stay."

“Thanks, Carl.”

We shook hands, and I entered the cozy room, pulled the blackout shades shut, fell into bed, and got a proper rest.

I woke up a few hours later and staggered out of bed. My eyes became narrow slits as I pulled the curtains open, and a wash of light bathed the room. When my eyes adjusted, I saw the pristine beach just outside the sliding glass door. There was a small patio area with two lounge chairs and a coffee table that opened to the white sand. Waves crashed on the shore and gulls hung in the air.

It was a nice room, and I knew the prices at the *Seven Seas* weren’t cheap. Big Carl had done me a solid.

I took a shower and put on my dirty clothes, then I tried to call Reagan, but the number was disconnected.

My face twisted with confusion.

It left me a little concerned. Why the hell would her phone be disconnected?

I left the *Seven Seas* and caught an Uber over to *Ray’s Cycle Universe.* My helmet, gloves, and leathers were all on the boat, along with my entire wardrobe. I had no personal belongings anymore, but my bike was still sitting in the parking lot at *Diver Down.*

The chime rang as I pushed into the dealership. New bikes glimmered under the lights, and the smell of fresh tires hit my nostrils.

"Hey, Tyson," Ray said. "How's it going?"

"It's going."

By the look on my face, Ray could tell I wasn't thrilled. "What did you do this time? Please tell me you didn't crash."

I chuckled. "No. No crashes. I need to get another helmet and gloves."

I told him what happened.

"You need another set of leathers?"

"I'll save that for when I actually have a closet to put them in."

He smiled. "Fair enough."

He made me a good deal, and I put the whole thing on a credit card. With my accounts un-frozen, and the money from my Hollywood sale firmly in the bank, cash flow wasn't an issue. But I had six figures in cash stuffed in a compartment on the *Wild Tide.* There was no doubt I would never see that money again. The thought of it just burned my ass.

Ray offered to have Jorge give me a ride back to *Diver Down.* Ray picked up the phone and dialed the service center extension. A few minutes later, Jorge pulled around front in a courtesy car. I thanked Ray, then hopped in the passenger seat. I was at *Diver Down* a few minutes later.

I strolled inside and took a seat at the bar. "Have you heard from Reagan?"

Madison shook her head.

"Her phone is disconnected."

She raised a curious eyebrow. "Maybe she didn't pay her bill?"

I shrugged.

“You stay with Jack last night?"

"Not really."

"You can always crash on my couch."

"I may take you up on that."

Sheriff Daniels called.

I knew it wasn't going to be good.

"When I suggested that you find probable cause to enter Declan's home, I meant *real* probable cause."

"JD heard a scream and believed a crime was in progress."

"I know. I've heard his bullshit story."

"We rescued a girl?"

"Who was there consensually," he added.

"Left unattended, she could have—"

Daniels cut me off. "Spare me the BS. Declan's out."

"What?" I exclaimed.

"He was arraigned this morning, and the judge tossed the charges."

"Why?"

"He's got a good attorney. The judge said the arresting officer didn't have probable cause to search the vehicle. Declan's suing the department for the damages to the house."

I frowned.

A call from a number I didn’t recognize flashed on the screen.

I usually didn't answer calls from unknown numbers, but it was an excuse to get off the phone with Daniels.

37

"Hello?"

"Hey, it's me," Reagan said.

"Did you get a new number?"

"Yeah. I had to separate myself from this whole thing. I was starting to get terrified of my phone, dreading the next call from the killer."

"So, you cut our line of communication with him?" I asked, a little upset.

"What was I supposed to do? I need to protect my mental sanity."

"I wish you would have talked to me before doing that."

"Oh, now I have to run all my personal life choices through you?"

"No," I said. "But have you ever stopped to consider the fact that our *friend* might not take too kindly to you cutting him off?"

She was silent for a moment.

"At least when he was calling you, we had some idea of what was going on."

"Well, I think he's calling the studio directly now. They've gotten several calls today."

"Has he left any messages?"

"Not yet."

"Where are you at?"

"The studio." She sighed. "I don't know. I just need a little distance from this whole thing.“

Someone shouted for Reagan. I could barely hear the voice that filtered through the phone in the background.

"Hang on just a sec," she said.

She had a brief exchange with someone, then a moment later, she grumbled. "Shit."

"What is it?"

"So much for distancing myself," Reagan said. "I just got another note. It was delivered by messenger."

"I'll be right there."

I left *Diver Down,* hopped on my bike, and zipped over to the television station. I signed in at the desk and found Reagan in the studio. A crowd hovered around her, peering at the note over her shoulder. Another cryptic message—the same format as the previous ones.

We found Elijah in an editing bay, working on the graphics for segment intros.

"How fast do you think you can decode this?" Reagan asked.

Elijah shrugged. "If he's using the same type of encryption, or something similar, maybe an hour? Maybe less? He's been using a pretty basic cipher. There are dozens of online resources for this type of stuff. He's not making something that's impossible to decode. He's just making us jump through hoops for his own amusement."

"You said this was delivered by messenger. What service?" I asked.

Reagan still had the 9x11 cardboard envelope. It had the logo of a local delivery company that was known for transporting small items around the island with same day service. Need food from a restaurant that didn't deliver? Call *Quick Key*. Need important documents sent across town? Call *Quick Key*. Didn't have time to grocery shop? Call *Quick Key*.

I called the delivery service to track the package. They should have had a record of who sent it, and the delivery person, but the woman on the phone assured me that no such delivery had been made. There was nothing in her system that showed a scheduled delivery to Reagan MacKenzie at the television station.

“Son-of-a-bitch," I grumbled to myself after I hung up the phone.

Reagan looked at me with concerned eyes. "What is it?"

"Do you have security footage on the premises?"

"Yeah."

"If I were a gambling man, and I am, I'd bet money that our killer delivered the message himself."

The color drained from Reagan's face. She looked horrified.

In the security suite, we were able to review the security camera footage. It was all high definition stuff—multiple feeds from various angles. Chuck was the lead security guard on the premises, and he helped us navigate through the footage.

The delivery guy wore a red cap, red shirt, and shorts. He had long curly hair. Sunglasses covered his eyes, and his face was obscured by the brim of his hat.

I was pretty sure the long hair was a wig.

"Do we have any footage of the parking lot?" I asked. "Maybe we can get a license plate number from his vehicle?"

Chuck scrolled through the footage. We saw the man enter and leave, but he walked onto the premises from around the corner. He wasn't in a vehicle.

"This guy is bold," Chuck said.

"Indeed, he is."

Reagan trembled slightly, unsettled by just how close the killer had gotten to her.

Her phone buzzed, and she swiped the screen. I heard a voice crackle through the speaker, but I couldn't make out what was said.

"Okay. Thanks. I'll be right there." Reagan looked to me. "Elijah cracked the cipher."

38

You changed your number. Does this mean we're not friends anymore? I so enjoyed our conversations. It's too bad. If you want to see what happens to people who aren't my friends, visit Angelfish Key.

If Reagan was unsettled before the note was decoded, she was even more so after.

"Just take a deep breath," I said.

"Is it too early to start drinking?" she asked, not entirely joking. "If he can walk into this building, he can reach me anywhere."

"I don't think he's going to try something like that again."

"How can you be so sure?"

"I think he just wanted to let you know that he can still communicate with you, even if you don't want to communicate with him."

Reagan grumbled.

I called Sheriff Daniels and filled him in.

"You and numb-nuts get down to the station, ASAP. We will take the patrol boat over to Angelfish Key and see what we can find."

"Copy that," I said.

By the look in Reagan's eyes, I could tell that she was dreading my leaving.

"I've got to go. Stay here. Don't go anywhere without an escort. Don't go home."

Reagan nodded and gave me a hug. She held on tight.

"It's going to be okay," I assured.

It was a promise that I had no control over.

I left the TV studio and raced across town to the Sheriff's Office. JD's red Porsche roared into the parking lot behind me. I pulled off my helmet and strapped it to the bike. I ran my fingers through my hair, trying to recover from helmet-head.

"What happened to you last night?" JD asked.

"The couch didn't offer a lot of support. I got a room at the *Seven Seas*."

"Scarlett didn't run you off, did she?"

"No," I lied.

"You know she's got a little crush on you?"

"I hadn't noticed."

JD scoffed. "You'd have to be blind not to notice. I think she's just trying to irritate me. It's not going to work though." He smiled. "I am a Zen master. Nothing that girl can do will upset me anymore." Then he added, "But you bang her, and I'll beat your ass."

"You don't have to worry about that."

The sheriff met us on the dock, and we boarded the patrol boat, along with Brenda and the forensics team.

Daniels cranked up the engines, and we idled out of the harbor. He brought the boat on plane and we skimmed across the surface, heading to Angelfish Key—an oasis of paradise that had now been sullied by the shadow of the *Sandcastle Killer.*

An hour later, we cruised into the secluded cove. Daniels idled the boat toward the beach, and JD and I hopped out in the surf. We trudged through the sand, scanning the pristine shore, looking for any sign of a body. We scoured the shoreline, the wooded areas, the hilltops—every square inch.

It took several hours.

We couldn't find a thing.

We just baked under the hot sun, sweating.

We combed the beach again, poking at the sand, looking for anything buried under the surface.

"I get the feeling he's fucking with us," JD said.

"I think you're right. But why send us on a wild goose chase? He's never done that before." A dreadful thought entered my mind. My stomach twisted. "Unless he wanted to get us out of Coconut Key."

"Why?" JD asked.

"Reagan." My jaw clenched tight and my hands balled into fists. "He's going after Reagan."

Daniels rounded up the team. We boarded the boat and raced back toward Coconut Key.

I hoped my hunch was wrong, but the sour, burning sensation in my stomach told me I had plenty to worry about.

39

As soon as I could get cell reception, I called Reagan. It went straight to voicemail.

My whole body tensed, and that sour feeling in the pit of my stomach intensified. We sliced through the water, plowing through the swells, spraying mists of salt-water into the air. The engines rumbled as we skimmed across the water.

I tried to act calm, but JD could see it in my eyes when we exchanged a glance.

I was worried.

I called Reagan several times during the trip back, but she never answered. I felt like a stalker. Maybe I was over-reacting?

When we arrived at the station, I hit the dock running and sprinted to the parking lot. I tried one more time to call Reagan to no avail, then hopped on my bike, pulled on my helmet, and cranked up the engine. I twisted the throttle, eased out the clutch, and launched out of the parking lot. The wind whistled through my helmet as I rode like a maniac to the television station.

I parked the bike by the entrance and dashed into the lobby. I lifted the visor to my helmet and asked the receptionist, "Is Reagan here?"

"I think she went home about an hour ago." My jaw tightened. I spun around, dashed out of the building, and hopped back on the bike. The engine roared as I raced to Reagan's house, carving around turns like I was racing the Isle of Man.

I parked the bike at the curb, sprinted up the walkway, and rang the bell. My heart pounded in my chest, and I heaved for breath.

I saw motion inside, and a moment later, Reagan pulled open the door. She didn't have chance to get a word out before I said, "I've been calling you for the last hour! Why haven't you called me back?"

Her face crinkled. "Getting a little needy, aren't you?" she asked in a sassy tone.

"I was worried about you."

"Aw, isn’t that special?"

My eyes narrowed at her.

She stepped aside and motioned for me to enter. She closed, and latched, the door behind me as I stepped into the foyer.

"I thought I told you to stay at the station?"

"You're not the boss of me."

"I thought you were the one who didn't want to be home alone?"

She shrugged. "Honestly, I don't think anywhere is safe. Might as well be at home. Besides, I bought this." She reached into her purse and pulled out a 9mm.

"Do you even know how to use that?"

"How hard can it be? You just point and pull the trigger, right?"

"That's a simplified version."

"You said you would take me to the range."

"I will."

She stuffed the weapon back into her purse.

Reagan grinned. "I think it's cute. You getting all protective."

She sauntered close and flung her arms around my neck. She gazed at me with those sparkling eyes. "Careful, Mr. Wild. I might start to think you care."

She reached up on her tiptoes and planted her full lips against mine.

A wave of relief washed through my body. I think I cared about this woman more than I wanted to admit.

Our lips broke apart for a moment.

"So why didn't you answer my call?"

"Because I left my phone in Patricia's car. She gave me a ride home from the station."

"What's the matter with your car?"

"I don't know. It wouldn't start."

I grimaced. Maybe it was a coincidence, or maybe the *Sandcastle Killer* had done something to her car? My mind swirled with paranoid conspiracies.

"I'm hesitant to ask, but what did you find on Angelfish Key?"

"Nothing."

Reagan's brow lifted with surprise. "Nothing? That's odd. Are you sure you looked hard enough?"

"We combed every inch of that island. Doesn't mean there's not a body there, but if there is, we couldn't find it. I think he's screwing with us."

Reagan deflated. "This is all my fault. I shouldn't have cut him off. He's angry."

"He's a control freak. That's why he abducts women and tortures them. It's all about control."

"Well, maybe since you didn't find the body, it means the girl is still alive?" she said with hopeful eyes.

"I don't know."

She paused for a moment, still clinging around me. "I liked this conversation better when we weren't talking. Can we go back to that part?"

"Not talking is good."

Our lips collided again in a passionate embrace.

Damn, she felt good in my arms! Our hips ground together, and our hands explored each other. Soon we were tugging at articles of clothing and peeling them off. We worked our way to the nearest hard surface, shedding garments like a snake sheds its skin.

I hoisted Reagan onto the kitchen counter, and she wrapped her magnificent legs around me. We went at it hot and heavy. The coffee pot rattled, and the cabinet doors quaked. Moans of ecstasy filled the kitchen, and she dug her nails into my back, and her hot sticky breath tickled my ears.

A day away from her, and I was a loaded weapon—and the safety was off.

I released all the tension and anxiety I had been carrying since Angelfish Key. When it was all over, our slick bodies clung together.

Neither one of us wanted to let go.

My heart swelled with emotion. I didn't know where this whole thing was going, but I sure wasn't going to let some psychopath take Reagan away from me.

The doorbell rang, startling both of us.

We scampered through the kitchen, naked, scooping up our clothes, trying to get dressed.

Reagan managed to pull her clothes on faster than I thought was physically possible. She adjusted her skirt and tried to compose herself as she sauntered toward the door. She fluffed her disheveled hair, put on a bright smile, then pulled the door open.

40

"You're quite popular. The phone has been buzzing the entire way over here," Patricia said.

Reagan swiped the screen on the device. She had dozens of missed calls and text messages.

She thanked Patricia, and the woman scampered down the walkway and jumped into her car, which was still running.

Reagan closed the door. When she turned around, her face was white as a ghost, and her eyes widened.

She showed me the display.

There was a text message that read: *[Did you really think I wouldn't be able to find your new number?]*

"That has to be him," she stammered.

Reagan scrolled through her missed calls. There were several voicemails from the same unknown number. She listened to one of them, then replayed the message for me on the speakerphone.

"I'm so disappointed in you," the killer said in a distorted voice. "I thought we had an understanding. We were so good together. I would have been loyal to you. Exclusive interviews. Rare insights into the mind of a maniac. You could have built a career off me. Now you'll die like the rest."

Reagan trembled.

My whole body tensed. I tried to soothe her fears. "He's just venting."

"What if he's not?"

I knew he was coming for Reagan, but I didn't want to alarm her. "As long as I'm around, he's not going to get anywhere near you."

There was no doubt that he had been watching Reagan. He knew when she was staying aboard the *Wild Tide,* and he knew when she was at home. He had to know about me, and perhaps that's why he sent us on the wild goose chase?

"I'm not trying to be the overprotective boyfriend, but you need to do what I say."

"So, you're my boyfriend?" Reagan asked, curiously.

I didn't reply to the question. "I'm just saying, you can't pretend this is a game. It's not. It's deadly serious for him. You're the person he can't control, and that's driving him insane."

"I've got news for him. Nobody can control me."

"I'm well aware of that."

Reagan sighed. "So what do we do?"

I thought about it for a moment. "Maybe it's best if you get out of Coconut Key for a while? Take a vacation?"

"No!" Reagan said. "I will not be forced out. I will not run away in fear."

There was a long moment of silence.

"What if we use this to our advantage?" she asked.

I didn't like where this was going. "How so?"

"We know he's angry with me. He threatened to kill me. I could be bait? You could spring a trap?"

"Absolutely not."

"Why not? I'll aggravate the shit out of him and draw him out."

The muscles in my jaw flexed.

Reagan's fingers danced across the screen and she clacked a text message, then sent it back to the killer.

"What did you just do?"

"What I do best," she said with a grin. "Get under people's skin."

I sighed, and my head fell into my hands. "What did you say?"

"I told him he was a pathetic little man."

"That's it?"

"I may have said he has a small dick and probably can't get it up."

"That should get under his skin, alright."

Reagan's antagonism didn't stop with her text message. She had a plan devised, and she asked me to escort her back to the television station. We caught a cab, and she pitched an idea for a segment on the evening news, and Harold agreed.

I watched the broadcast from the soundstage. I was ready and waiting for the dirt-ball to show up, but he seemed too smart to do something rash.

He hadn't responded to Reagan's messages. He was a cool customer. Maybe Reagan overestimated her ability to rattle him? Beware of the quiet ones... they get you when you least expect it. The killer was certainly being quiet.

"Tonight, we have a special segment with our very own Reagan MacKenzie," Emma Steele said, introducing her.

"Thank you, Emma," Reagan said, then addressed the camera. "A few days ago, we aired a broadcast that contained a long conversation with a man who claims to be the *Sandcastle Killer.* My hope was that we might gain valuable insight into his sadistic mind? Perhaps we would learn clues that might lead to his capture and save future victims from a horrible fate? Many viewers were outraged that we provided the killer with an opportunity to be heard. While I do not apologize for, or regret, my actions, I feel that I can no longer, in good conscience, amplify the killer's message. I will not provide the ego boost that he so desperately craves.

"He is a despicable man who has no social value. He lacks the guts and courage to be a functional member of society. He hides in the shadows, preying on the vulnerable. He has threatened me personally for refusing to cover his story any longer. So, if you're watching, Mr. Sandcastle... I beg you to release your current victim. Come get me instead. I dare you! I am not afraid. We are not afraid. The citizens of Coconut Key will no longer live in fear. It is you who will be hunted from now on."

The cameras cut back to Emma. She had a shocked look on her face. She forced a smile and looked into the camera and said, "Well, that's quite a challenge. Will it be accepted? Stay tuned, we'll be right back after these messages."

The production manager shouted, "And, we're out to commercial."

Like a hive of bees, production assistants buzzed about.

Reagan disconnected from the wireless microphone and stepped away from the anchor desk.

"You've got some balls, honey," Emma said. "I'll give you that."

Reagan strutted to me, looking like she had just guzzled a pot of coffee. Her eyes were wide, and she trembled slightly. She was in a heightened state from the adrenaline. "Well, what do you think?"

"I think you're insane."

"A girl has to have a little crazy in her to keep things interesting."

"I think you have more than a little crazy in you. Certainly interesting, that's for sure."

She raised on her tiptoes and kissed me on the cheek and took my hand. "Don't worry. I have full faith and confidence in you. I know you'll keep me safe."

I gave her a sideways glance. "No pressure."

41

The battery terminal had been disconnected. That's why Reagan's car didn't start earlier. It was a quick fix, and the vehicle turned over with ease once reconnected. It made me wonder if the killer had tampered with it?

A swarm of reporters from other news stations crowded around Reagan's house. They mobbed the car as we pulled into the driveway.

They shoved microphones in her face, and the blinding camera lights caused her eyes to squint as she stepped from the vehicle. The normally quiet neighborhood was full of news vans with satellite dishes on top. Neighbors crowded around, watching the circus.

Everyone in Coconut Key had seen her broadcast.

Reagan pushed toward the front door, and I weaved through the horde behind her. They shouted questions like, "Do you think the killer will come after you now?"

"Now that you've antagonized the killer, do you think the body count will rise?"

“Is the sheriff providing added protection for you? And how will the diversion of resources affect the community at large?"

Reagan didn't answer.

"Do you think your challenge to the killer was irresponsible?"

Reagan forced her way to the door, put her key into the slot, and twisted the handle. She pushed inside, and I followed. Reagan latched the deadbolt, locking out the world behind us.

The reporters hovered around the front door, each one trying to wrap up their segment.

Reagan looked frazzled. The lights, cameras, microphones, and invasive questions could feel claustrophobic and overwhelming.

"Fucking vultures!” Reagan said as she exhaled.

I smirked at the irony.

Reagan moved into the kitchen, grabbed a bottle of bourbon, and poured two glasses. She handed one to me, and we toasted. "To poor decisions."

We clinked glasses, and I sipped the amber liquid.

"Pissing off a serial killer may not have been one of your brighter moments," I said.

She frowned at me. "When you catch this guy because of me, I'll expect a formal retraction of that statement."

Reagan's phone dinged with text messages and notifications. Her face was buried into the screen as she scrolled through her social media profiles. A slight grin curled on her face. "Wow, looks like I really lit things up on the Interwebs."

She read a list of comments:

"Wow, you're so brave!"

"You're one bad-ass bitch!"

"I hope you get that bastard!"

"You go, girl."

"Just another ho gonna get hosed."

Reagan moved to the window and peered at the horde of reporters still lingering in her yard. Her face scrunched up. "Look at them. You know, they're just going to pick up the slack where I left off. He'll get all the media coverage he wants. He doesn't need me. Refusing to cover him isn't going to change anything."

I could tell Reagan was a little disillusioned with her industry.

Jack called. "Seems like your girl went off the deep end!"

"You saw the show?" I asked.

"I saw her paint a target on herself. I'm guessing you're not going to get much sleep tonight?"

"The sheriff's doubling patrols in the area. I don't think the killer would be bold enough to strike here at the house, but I'm going to fix a pot of coffee and take firewatch."

"I'm more than happy to take the second shift. I'll take a cat nap now and call you around 2 AM."

"Thanks, I appreciate it."

"Anytime, brother."

I hung up the phone and slid the device back into my pocket.

I moved to the alarm panel in the foyer. It was lifeless. "Does this thing work?"

"No. Came with the house. Previous owner. I've been meaning to call and get service connected. There's something wrong with the main power supply. I think the backup battery is dead too. I don't even know where it is."

I sighed and shook my head.

I strolled through the house, checking the doors and windows, making sure everything was secured. The windows were all closed and locked. But I found an area of concern—a sliding glass door in the living room that opened to a patio with the beach beyond.

It was unlocked.

My jaw clenched. "Did you leave this door unlocked?"

Reagan shrugged. "I don't know. Maybe?" She thought about it for a moment. "I was out on the patio this morning. Maybe I forgot?"

I grumbled under my breath. "You need to be more careful."

"Yes, sir," she said with a mock salute.

I glared at her.

There was another sliding glass door in her bedroom. They were notoriously easy to defeat. A burglar could lift them out of their tracks, and the spring-loaded locking mechanism would typically release. You could use all sorts of double-bolt locking mechanisms, or security rods in the tracks, but none of those would stop a well-placed brick.

I slid open the door, strolled down to the beach, and surveyed the area. Stars flickered overhead, the breeze blew through my hair, and waves crashed against the shore. It was a security nightmare. Multiple escape routes for a criminal.

I went back to the house and fixed a pot of coffee. It was going to be a long night, and I needed to stay sharp. I shouldn't have had a glass of whiskey.

"What are you going to do?" Reagan asked. "Stay up all night?"

"JD said he would take a shift."

"And how long can you do that for? A couple days? A week?"

I shrugged. "As long as I have to."

"You're not a machine."

"Maybe you should have thought about that before you dared him to come get you?" I smiled.

She scowled at me, playfully.

The coffee pot percolated on the counter. I poured myself a mug and mixed in cream and sugar, then we watched a movie.

I made routine checks around the house throughout the

evening. Everything was secure, and the neighborhood seemed calm. The reporters had all left.

Around midnight, we moved to the bedroom, and Reagan settled in for the night.

I sat in a chair next to the bed.

She looked at me like I was crazy. "You're really going to stay up all night long?"

I nodded.

"Come to bed."

It was usually an offer I wouldn’t refuse. "I want to be ready if he strikes."

“Don’t I get a goodnight kiss?” she asked in a pouty voice.

I tucked Reagan in, but I didn't allow myself to get too distracted by her charms. I didn't want to get caught with my pants down, so to speak.

She finally nodded off after some tossing and turning, and I tried to keep myself awake. My head dipped a few times as the evening dragged on, but I caught myself before dozing off. It was 2:20 AM when JD texted. *[Just woke up. Overslept. I'll be there in 30.]*

[Okay.]

[How goes it?]

[All is quiet on the homefront.]

I was about to get up and do my routine patrol around the premises when I heard a noise in the living room. A spike of adrenaline rushed through me. I sprang from the chair, drew my pistol, and edged down the hallway with my weapon in the firing position. I moved through the shadows, ready to blast. An eerie feeling washed over me, and the hairs on the back of my neck stood tall. I had that uncanny sensation that I always had right before making contact with the enemy.

42

I breathed a sigh of relief when I saw the source of the noise. The breeze from the ceiling fan had blown a utility bill off the counter. It clacked against the floor and was fluttering in the breeze by the time I stepped into the living room.

I holstered my pistol, moved toward the counter, and bent over to pick up the piece of paper from the tile.

As I stood up and set it on the counter, I saw a shadow dance across the wall.

There was someone behind me.

I reached for my gun and spun around, but by that time, it was too late.

An aluminum bat swooshed through the air and connected with my head.

Ping!

The blow rattled my skull, damn near taking my head off. It

twisted me around, and I tumbled to the ground. Crimson blood spewed from my lips. My vision doubled, and pain jolted down my spine.

The pain was so intense, I went numb.

I tried to focus my thoughts, but I was somewhere in that gray area of consciousness.

A blurry figure pounced on top of me. Then he stabbed a syringe into my flesh. He pushed the plunger, and I felt a cool sensation flowing into my neck.

Then everything went black.

I don't know how long I was out, but when I awoke, JD was hovering over me, shaking my shoulder and snapping his fingers in front of my face.

My vision was still blurry as hell. "What happened?"

The words slurred out of my fat lips. It felt like I had just gotten back from the dentist. My jaw was swollen, and my neck ached. My temples throbbed.

It hurt to exist.

"Looks like someone got a hell of a sucker punch in?"

"Reagan. Where's Reagan?"

I could see well enough to make out JD's grim frown. He shook his head. "She's gone."

I staggered to my feet, and JD took hold of my arm to steady me.

"Easy there, cowboy."

I brushed him off and staggered into the bedroom. The disheveled sheets left an imprint where Reagan had been.

The sliding glass door was open, and the breeze fluttered the curtains.

I dashed onto the patio and trudged to the beach. I stumbled and fell in the sand, then pulled myself up. The ground was uneasy beneath my feet, and the world spun slightly.

I glanced around, but I couldn't see shit. My vision was too blurry to make out anything in the distance. Waves crashed against the shore, and the inky blackness of the ocean loomed like a void waiting to swallow me whole.

JD caught up with me. "I think we need to get you to the hospital. Have you checked out."

"No. I've got to find Reagan."

"You're not gonna be good to anybody if your brain swells and you end up incapacitated. I'm taking you to the emergency room."

My jaw involuntarily clinched, sending a spike of pain through my body. I wanted to scream, and I did.

That hurt like hell too.

I was so mad, my eyes welled, and my throat tightened. "He must have been in the house the whole time."

"What?" JD asked.

"When we came home from the station. The sliding door was unlocked. He must have been hiding in a closet, waiting."

"Damn. That's messed up."

"I know."

My mouth had that tinny, metallic taste of blood. I tongued a molar on my left side. It wiggled more than I would have liked.

JD called Sheriff Daniels and told him what happened, then we hopped into his car and drove to the emergency room.

I was triaged by the same nurse who attended to JD the last time we were in here. "You're a familiar face. I don't like to see familiar faces."

I pointed at Jack. "It was him last time, not me."

"Yeah, but you look worse than he did."

The whole side of my face was black, blue, and purple. There was blood in my left eye, and my jaw ached so bad I thought it was broken.

After the nurse assessed me, I was taken to a room in the ER.

They did the usual bit of starting IV fluids and hooking me up to the monitors.

"Just couldn't stay away, could you?" Dr. Parker asked upon entering the room.

I looked at him flatly and explained the situation.

"Tell me, did you have any loss of consciousness?" he asked.

"I think so, yes. But that was mainly due to a substance the attacker injected."

"What do you think that substance could have been?"

"I don't know. You're the doctor. You tell me?"

"I'll run a toxicology screening." He made a note. "Have you had any nausea or vomiting?"

I shook my head. It hurt.

"What about grogginess, clumsiness?"

"I got hit with an aluminum bat. Yes. I'm a little groggy."

"Sensitivity to light?" he asked, shining a penlight in my eyes.

I squinted.

I wanted to shove the penlight up his ass.

"How about confusion or disorientation?"

"Other than when I first woke up, no."

I'm going to ask you some basic questions to gauge your cognitive response. Where were you when the incident happened?"

"I was at Reagan MacKenzie's house."

His eyes perked up. "Ooh, I like her. Daring."

My eyes narrowed at him.

"How did you get to the hospital?"

"JD took me."

"Do you feel dizzy now?"

I nodded.

"What about blurred vision?"

“It's not as bad as it was. But it's not perfect."

He scribbled notes in my file, then said. "I think you probably have a mild concussion. I'd like to do a brain scan and an x-ray. Rule out a brain bleed, swelling, broken bones, anything that might need our immediate attention."

He ordered the scans, and a tech escorted me to radiology. They took multiple views of my neck and skull, then did a CT scan.

I asked the tech how everything looked, but he wasn't at liberty to say. "The doctor will go over the results with you shortly. But I can confirm, you do have a brain."

"That's debatable," I said.

43

A nurse gave me an ice pack for my jaw. I was starting to look like a chipmunk. Dr. Parker took his time getting back to me with my results. The ER didn't look *that* crowded when we came in, but it took him about 45 minutes to make his way back around. He studied my chart as he entered the room. Maybe the toxicology screening took longer?

"I don't see any indication of brain trauma, bleeding, or swelling. That's good news. No broken bones or fractures. I think you're just suffering from a mild concussion and a lot of bruising. You need to stay awake for the next several hours, and you should have someone stay with you to monitor your condition. If you start getting dizzy, nauseous, or your vision worsens, I need to see you back here."

"What about the tox report?"

"The substance your attacker injected you with was likely propofol."

"That's a sedative, right?" I asked.

Dr. Parker nodded. "It's commonly used in surgery settings. It can knock a person out quickly, but the effects are short lasting."

"Where would someone acquire that?"

"Look around. This hospital is full of it. There are probably vials of it in the cabinets behind me," he said pointing.

"You don't keep that stuff locked up?" I asked.

"It's not a controlled substance. There's a low potential for abuse. I know some hospitals are tightening up with it, but we haven't had a problem here. Vials haven't been going missing, I don't think. Pharmacy checks for discrepancies everyday. I'm not going to say it's impossible, but it would be hard for someone to steal drugs from this facility."

I thought about it for a moment.

"I'll get your discharge orders ready. You can get out of here shortly." Parker turned to the door.

"Excuse me, Doc. Can I get a list of everyone in this facility with access to that drug?"

He looked at me like I was crazy. His brow knitted together. "You don't think someone from this facility is..."

I shrugged. "I'm not about to rule anything out."

"Do you have a warrant for that information?"

"If you want to play it that way, I can get it. But it would be a lot easier if you would just let me look at your personnel files."

"That's really above my pay grade. You'll need to talk to the administration office. That's an HR thing. I don't know if we're allowed to share employment data. I just fix sick people."

"No offense, Doc, but you can't fix dead people. Reagan MacKenzie was abducted tonight, and every second I have to screw around with red-tape brings her another second closer to death. You understand that? You took an oath to help people. To save lives. You have an opportunity to save many right now."

Parker's face tensed. He was silent for a long moment. "Can you walk? Are you steady on your feet?"

I nodded.

He waved the file folder toward the door. "Come with me."

JD helped me lower the railing on the hospital bed. The bag of IV fluids was on a rolling stand. I took it with me and followed the doctor down the hallway, wearing the ridiculous green gown with my ass crack half hanging out.

He led me to the nurses' station, and we walked around the counter to a computer terminal. He entered his passcode and brought up the screen.

"What, specifically, are you looking for?"

"White male. 30s. Former military background. I'm guessing special operations combat medic. Probably a new hire. Last few months."

Dr. Parker's face went pale.

"Sound familiar?"

"That sounds like Erik Cain." Parker said. Then he dismissed it. "Can't be. One of the nicest guys I've ever met.

Knowledgeable, dedicated. The kind of guy that would do anything for you."

"Pull up his information."

Parker tapped a few keys and brought up the personnel file of Erik Cain. I grabbed a pen and a post-it note and scribbled down his name and address. It was a box number at *Salt Point Marina.*

"You really think that's him? The Sandcastle Killer?" Parker asked in a hushed tone.

"Is he working tonight?"

Parker shook his head. "No. Looks like he's on the schedule for tomorrow night."

"If you see him, or talk to him, call me immediately, and don't say a word. Do not share this with anyone else. Is that clear?"

Parker nodded.

"Lives are at stake." I wrote my contact information on a post-it.

JD and I exchanged a glance.

"Let's go find that son-of-a-bitch," I said.

44

We left the ER, and I kept an ice pack planted against my jaw and neck, alternating a few minutes on, a few minutes off.

Every time JD shifted gears in the Porsche, the jolt threw my neck a little, sending a slight twinge of pain down my spine.

Joy.

We headed across the island to the Salt Point Marina. The sky began to lighten as the sun crept up on the horizon. I had that tired, thin feeling, but was spiked up on adrenaline at the same time. My nerves tingled and my head throbbed.

With the top down, the wind whistled through the cockpit and blew through my hair. I pulled my phone from my pocket and called Brenda. It wasn't quite 7 AM yet.

"Did you find any trace of propofol in any of the victims?"

"If I recall correctly, there were no blood concentrations, but the full toxicology report hasn't come back yet. That stuff clears the system pretty quickly."

"How quickly?"

"I think the half-life is 12 hours. Should be out completely within three days."

"The killer seems to be holding on to his victims for at least a week before he disposes of them," I said. "I think that's by design."

"You think he's using the drug to subdue his victims when he acquires them?"

"I'm absolutely positive." I didn't go into details about the attack.

I thanked her for her advice and called the sheriff's office. A deputy gave me the registration information for Erik Cain's boat. It was named *On the Hook.*

Salt Point was a harbor for commercial fishing boats. There were shrimp boats and several large commercial fishing charters. There were a few liveaboards mixed in. Crews were prepping the boats, getting ready for the day.

I climbed out of JD's Porsche and made my way to the office. An old man sat behind the counter eating a donut, watching the morning news. He didn't have much hair on top, but what he did have on the sides was gray, and he had a long gray beard that was stained yellow from tobacco smoke. He had a bulbous nose and rosy cheeks, and the faded tattoo on his forearm told me that he was in the Navy once. I figured that he probably worked on the fishing boats at one point in time, and now made his living sitting behind this counter, collecting rent, troubleshooting tenant issues, and keeping the property maintained.

"Do you know where I can find the *On the Hook?*" I asked.

"Erik's boat?" the man asked.

I nodded. "I'll show you."

He climbed out of his chair and ambled around the counter. He seemed eager to get up and do something—anything to break up the monotony.

"You friends of Erik's?"

JD flashed his badge.

The man's eyes widened with concern. "He's not in any kind of trouble, is he?"

JD and I exchanged a glance.

"We just need to ask him a few questions," I said.

"The name's Buck," the man said.

We introduced ourselves.

"What the hell happened to your face?" Buck asked.

"He got in a fight with a baseball bat and lost," JD said.

"What happened? Did you piss off your girlfriend?"

"No," I said. "Nothing like that."

"My wife came at me with a baseball bat once," Buck said.

My eyes widened. "What happened?"

"Lost these two teeth." He pulled his cheek back and smiled wide, displaying the gap where his molars *should* have been.

"What did you do?" JD asked.

"Her sister," Buck said with a grin.

“Was it worth it?” JD asked.

“Well, this was after we were divorced, mind you. See, I caught her cheating on me with my best friend. I had to get a little payback. So, yeah, I guess it was worth it—just to see the look on her face.”

Buck shuffled down the dock to Erik’s slip—it was empty.

"Have any idea where he might be?" I asked.

Buck shrugged. "I'm not the nosy sort."

"What can you tell me about Erik?” I asked.

"Great guy. Do anything for you. Pays his rent on time. Doesn't cause trouble. What did you say this was about again?"

I smiled. "Just routine."

Buck's suspicious eyes narrowed. "That means he done something. Or, you think he done something."

"Have you noticed anything odd about his behavior?" I asked.

"Like I said, I try not to notice my tenants."

"Thanks, Buck."

We shook hands, and the old man strolled back to the office.

"Call your buddy at the Coast Guard," I said to JD. "We'll sit and wait for Erik to come back. The Coast Guard can search his boat."

The Coast Guard could search a boat on the water for any

reason, or no reason at all. Under the guise of national security, there was no Fourth Amendment on the water.

JD made a few phone calls, and a small patrol boat showed up within half an hour. It was a 25 foot *Defender* class boat with an aluminum hull and an orange foam-filled floatation collar. There was a crew of three.

Lieutenant Commander Henley stepped off the boat and greeted us on the dock. "I was told you boys need a little assistance?"

"We're looking at a suspect in the *Sandcastle* killings," I said.

The lieutenant commander's eyes widened. "Really?"

I nodded. "We were hoping you could board the suspect's boat and search for anything incriminating?"

"No problem. Where's the boat?"

"That's the problem. We don't know when, or if, he's coming back. But I don't think he knows we're on to him."

"We're happy to help," Henley said.

“It may be a while."

“If I get an emergency call, we gotta take it."

"Understood," I said.

"Where do you want us?" the lieutenant commander asked. "We could stay here, but if your suspect pulls in to the marina and sees us, he might get spooked."

"Agreed."

"I'm sure we can find a place to hide not far from here, then pull him over on the water."

I told him the name of Erik's boat. Henley gave me his cell phone number, and asked me to call him if we had visual contact with *On the Hook.*

The only thing we could do now was sit back and wait.

45

I drank cup after cup of coffee in the office, pacing back and forth. I couldn't sit still. My head throbbed and swelled like a pumpkin. But it was nothing compared to the anger that swelled in my heart. I wanted to catch this son-of-a-bitch and rip him from limb to limb.

The morning sun crested the horizon, glimmering across the water. The harbor looked picturesque. Boats gently swayed with the swells. Gulls squawked in the air. It was always hard to fathom how such grim things could happen in this paradise.

Isabella answered when I called. "I'm guessing you need another favor?"

"I need you to track another phone."

"Tyson, when are you going to give me something challenging?"

"Challenging? You couldn't track the last phone I gave you."

“Whatever,” she groaned. “That was a special circumstance. I’ll find this one.”

I gave her Erik’s cell phone number that the hospital had on file.

Isabella hung up and called me back 20 minutes later. "Okay, maybe I spoke too soon. I can't find it. The phone is probably off. It's not pinging the cell towers."

I clenched my jaw, then winced from the pain. "Can you give me the location history from that cell phone?"

"That's a little trickier," Isabella said. "I’d need direct access to the phone. Or, I can send a text message to the target device. The user would then have to click a link which would download an app. Most people know not to do that."

"Can you mask the number?"

"Sure. But there're no guarantees. Depends on how savvy the person is and how security conscious."

"They're savvy."

"Can you get access to the device?"

"If I could access the device, would I be calling you to track it?"

She huffed. "No need to get sassy." She paused. "I'll call you if the device shows up on the network."

"Thank you."

She hung up, and I slipped my phone into my pocket.

"I'm guessing this isn't about unpaid parking tickets," Buck said.

"No, it's a little more serious than that," I said.

It was 10:33 AM when Erik's boat pulled into the marina. The Coast Guard Defender entered behind him.

Erik pulled *On the Hook* into the slip and tied off the boat. The lieutenant commander shouted at him through a bull-horn. "United States Coast Guard. Prepare to be boarded for routine inspection!"

Erik looked at them like they were crazy.

JD and I sprinted out of the office and jogged down the dock. We arrived at the *On the Hook* about the time Henley boarded the boat with another officer.

"I'm in port," Erik protested. "You can't come on my boat without a warrant?"

"I'm afraid we can," Henley said.

A third officer kept his assault rifle shouldered and aimed at Erik.

The two officers pushed into the salon and rooted around.

Erik stood in the cockpit with his hands in the air. We stood on the dock and watched the whole thing go down. Erik's curious eyes glanced to us, wondering what the hell was going on.

JD flashed his badge. "Coconut County Sheriff. We'd like to have a few words with you."

"You want to tell me what this is about?" he growled.

"Where have you been?" Jack asked.

"That's none of your goddamn business."

"Oh, I'd say it is."

"Where were you last night?" I asked.

"Am I under arrest?"

"Got something!" Henley shouted from within the cabin.

He emerged a moment later wearing latex gloves, holding a bloody rope, a hunting knife, and a roll of duct tape.

"You are now," I said, drawing my weapon.

"What for?"

"Murder, kidnapping... I'm sure I'll think of a few other things," I said. "Step off the boat and get down on the ground. Facedown, hands upon your head."

Erik scowled at me, then reluctantly complied. "This is bull-shit. I'm gonna sue the department for wrongful imprisonment."

"Give it your best shot, cupcake," JD said as I latched the cuffs around Erik's wrists.

I wasn't nice about it. I slapped them against the bone as hard as I could, then ratcheted them tight.

The other Coast Guard officer stepped into the cockpit with a box of hypodermic needles. “Found these?”

JD and I exchanged a glance.

“Definitely log those as evidence," I said.

JD and I yanked Erik from the dock. He was a big boy—6’1”, 220 lbs. Thick with muscle.

The Coast Guard collected the evidence, then transferred

the items into the custody of the Coconut County Sheriff's Department after all the paperwork was done.

I called Sheriff Daniels, and he met us at the marina in the patrol car. We stuffed Erik in the back, then followed Daniels back to the station.

The sheriff knew better than to leave me alone in an interrogation room with the perp. Erik was smart enough to keep his mouth shut, and if I had been alone with him, I would have beat a confession out of him. As it stood, Erik sat in the tiny room with a smug grin on his face.

"Where is Reagan MacKenzie?" I asked.

"I'll be happy to answer any of your questions in the presence of my attorney. Until that time, I am asserting my Fifth Amendment privilege." He smiled.

My hands balled into fists, and rage boiled under my skin. It was all I could do not to bust his nose or break his jaw.

I owed him some payback.

Daniels shut down the session as soon as Erik asked for an attorney. We regrouped in the hallway.

"We confiscated all of his personal belongings during processing," Daniels said. "I've got the tech team making a disk image of the hard drive from his cell phone. Nothing we get off that will be admissible, but it might point us in the direction of Reagan MacKenzie. I've also got them analyzing the bloodstains on the rope. Hopefully we can figure out who that belongs to and link it to one of the victims."

"A case of whiskey says I can get into that phone in less than five minutes," I said.

Sheriff Daniels looked skeptical. After a moment, he said, "You're on."

46

I didn't specify how I'd get the data. My method was certainly going to piss Daniels off.

I stormed into the interrogation room with the cell phone.

Erik sat there with that smug grin on his face, waiting for his attorney. "I'm still not talking to you."

I cocked my fist back and swung as hard as I could. My knuckles slammed against his cheekbone, twisting his head to the side. The smack echoed off the tiny walls, and blood sprayed from his lips.

It felt good to hit the bastard.

I'd probably pay for it later, but the momentary satisfaction was worth it.

While Erik was disoriented, I grabbed his finger and placed it on the biometric scanner on the phone. The screen unlocked, and I immediately went into the settings and turned off the password protection.

Erik growled at me. "You can't do that!"

"I just did."

I stormed out of the interrogation room, and Sheriff Daniels glared at me in the hallway.

I handed him the device. "I'll take a case of *Roses & Thorns* single barrel."

The sheriff's eyes narrowed at me.

"Have the crime lab pull the location history of this device and search it for anything that might coincide with body dump sites, the television station, Reagan's house, etc. Look for texts, pictures, emails, anything that may be able to tie him to one of the victims. "

"That son-of-a-bitch is gonna sue the department over what you just did," Daniels growled.

I shrugged, innocently. "What? I just gave him a chiropractic neck adjustment."

The veins in the sheriff's temples throbbed.

"He fell during the initial arrest," JD said. "That's how he sustained his injuries."

I smiled "What he said."

"This better lead to something," Daniels said.

We waited around for the tech guys to pull the data and analyze it. I continued to load up on coffee and stuff donuts into my mouth, pacing around the office. I kept popping ibuprofen like it was candy. I was a crazed zombie, staggering around the office, sleep deprived, sore, and pissed off.

"Try to relax," JD said. "Why don't you get some sleep?"

"I can't sleep!"

"I'm sure she's okay," JD said. He could see the concern in my eyes.

"I think Reagan is far from okay."

"His pattern has been to hang onto his victims. I don't think she's..." He didn't want to finish the sentence.

I took a deep breath.

"We'll find her," he assured.

I felt completely helpless. There was nothing I could do.

"As long as we have that bastard in custody," JD said, "we know there's still hope."

"I just hope we find something that ties him definitively to these murders. Otherwise he's going to walk."

It wasn't long after that when Sheriff Daniels approached with the bad news. "You're not gonna like this."

My jaw tensed.

"The location history on the cell phone is a bust. The data doesn't correlate to any of the sites where we found victim remains. It mostly places Erik at the hospital, or in the marina. There are a lot of gaps in the data where he apparently shut the phone off. I think it's safe to say our suspect is smart enough not to leave his cell phone on when he's committing heinous acts."

"What about the rope and the knife?" I asked.

"The blood on the rope doesn't match any of the victims. It seems to be his blood."

I grumbled under my breath.

"His attorney is here and is pitching a fit. We've got nothing on this guy."

"Everything about him fits the profile," I said. "Hell, he had syringes on his boat."

"Which he claims he uses for testosterone replacement therapy." Daniels said. "There were no traces of propofol in any of the syringes, and none found on his boat. He's got a prescription for TRT. So, he juices a little? I can't arrest him for that."

Anger boiled within me.

"Until we have something concrete, I have to cut him loose," Daniels said. "But stay on top of him. Follow him around. He'll know you're watching, and my guess is he won't step out of line."

My stomach twisted. It was bad news for Reagan. "If Reagan is still alive, and he has her stashed somewhere, he won't risk going back to the site while we have him under surveillance. She'll die out there."

"So you better find her before she does," Daniels said.

Erik's attorney escorted him through the station. The handcuffs had carved deep grooves into his skin, and the scumbag rubbed his wrists. He flashed a cocky smile at JD and I as he passed.

"Your officers assaulted my client," the attorney growled. "He'd like to press charges."

The sheriff's jaw tightened, and his eyes narrowed. "I can assure you, my officers would never use unnecessary force. It's not uncommon for suspects to fall and injure themselves while in handcuffs. They have no way to brace themselves against a fall. Can lead to some pretty nasty cuts and bruises on the face."

The attorney knew better. He'd heard the story several times before. “Don’t give me that bullshit. You illegally searched his mobile device.”

"If you want to file frivolous charges, that is your prerogative," Daniels said.

The attorney exchanged a glance with his client.

Erik smiled. "I don't think charges are necessary at this time. The officers were just doing their job. I'm actually glad they're so zealous. We need to keep the streets of Coconut Key clean."

Erik flashed a smug grin, then strolled out the front door with his attorney. He was a free man, for now.

47

We tailed Erik around for the rest of the day, then I had to concede the fact that I was, indeed, mortal.

I needed sleep.

Daniels sent two deputies to take over our surveillance operation, and JD dropped me off at Reagan's house. I secured the premises, made an ice pack, and crawled into her bed. Her sweet perfume lingered on the pillow. I breathed her in, and the pit of my stomach twisted. A mix of rage and sadness swirled within me. I had to acknowledge the possibility that I might never see her again.

But I didn't entertain that thought for too long.

My mind raced, and my body vibrated with adrenaline. I was overtired, and I found it hard to settle down. When I finally nodded off, the morning came all too soon. The sun blasted through the blinds. The entire night had passed, and I hadn't moved so much as a muscle. My bladder was about to explode.

When I sat up, I was reminded just how stiff and sore I was. The bathroom mirror gave me a grim picture of myself. The black and blue bruises had blossomed into shades of green, yellow, and purple. I looked like something out of a horror movie.

In the kitchen, I fumbled through the fridge, looking for something to eat. There wasn't much—sour milk and eggs, way past their expiration date.

I got dressed, grabbed my helmet and gloves, and was about to hop on the bike and head to the *Driftwood* diner when Sheriff Daniels called. "Get down to the station, ASAP!"

"What's going on?"

"Two guys fishing near Barracuda Key picked up a young girl in the water, clinging to a shipping pallet. I think she may be one of the *Sandcastle's* intended victims."

"I'm on my way."

I hopped on the bike and zipped across town.

JD met me at the station.

We raced down the dock and boarded the sheriff's patrol boat and headed out to sea to rendezvous with the fishing boat. An ocean rescue paramedic team followed us. We skimmed across the surface, spraying mists of saltwater. The engines roared, and the boat bounced across the swells.

"What do we know?" I shouted over the engines.

"Not much," Daniels said. "It looks like she'd been at sea for several days, drifting."

We found the fishermen not far from Barracuda Key island.

They were in a 35 foot *MegaMarine* sport-fish.

We pulled alongside and boarded the boat, and the paramedics went to work evaluating the girl.

She sat in the salon, wrapped in a blanket. Her blonde hair was tangled and matted from several days in the ocean. Her once fair skin was now red and peeling from the sun. She looked like a burn victim.

The paramedics checked her vitals and started IV fluids.

The girl was severely dehydrated.

Tim, the owner of the boat said, “We found her drifting in the water. It was a miracle that we even saw her."

I knelt down beside the girl. “I'm Tyson. I'm a deputy with the Coconut County Sheriff's Department. What's your name?"

Her empty eyes stared into space. She had the look of someone who had been through a severe trauma. Eyes as deep as oceans. It took her a moment to speak, and when she did, it was faint. "Heather."

"Can you tell me what happened, Heather?"

"I don't really remember," she said in a scratchy, weak voice. "One minute, I was in Coconut Key, the next minute I woke up on a boat, tied up."

“What happened then?”

“I was brought to an island and..."

Her eyes welled with tears and she began sobbing. "It was horrible. I thought I was going to die. I was sure he was going to kill me."

"Who?"

"I don't know. I never saw his face. He wore a mask."

"How did you get off the island?"

She took a moment to compose herself. "He'd leave me alone for days at a time. I managed to untie myself, and I found a pallet that I thought I could use as a raft. I had to get off that island. Anything was better than staying there. I figured if I died at sea, so what? It was better than dying there."

"You're safe now. You're gonna be all right. He can't hurt you anymore." I paused. "Where are you from?"

"Miami."

"What were you doing in Coconut Key?"

"I needed to get away. I was involved in some bad shit in Miami. I thought I could start over in Coconut Key." A grim chuckle barely escaped her lips. "Some new start, huh?"

"You have any family in the area?"

She shook her head.

"Where are your folks?"

"Oklahoma. But we don't talk."

It explained why no one reported her missing.

She stopped crying, and her face grew solemn. Rage and hatred filled her eyes. Her lips quivered as she said, "You're gonna get that fucker, right?"

"I promise, we will," I assured. "Was there anyone else on the island?"

"I don't think so. Once I got free, I got the hell out of there as fast as I could."

"How long have you been at sea?"

"Three days, I think."

"Do you know where the island is?" I asked.

She shook her head.

"What can you tell me about it?"

"It was run down. It must have been an old resort. There were several cabins. There was an old pool that was full of algae. Everything was rotting and dilapidated."

I knew instantly where she was talking about. I exchanged a glance with JD. "Sounds like the old resort at Crystal Key."

I thanked Heather for the information and wished her well. The paramedics transferred her onto the rescue boat and took her back to the hospital in Coconut Key.

We boarded the sheriff's patrol boat and raced toward Crystal Key.

It had once been a posh resort, but it had been abandoned for the last few years. The previous hurricane had demolished the property. I guess it was underinsured, and the owners filed bankruptcy. The property had been on the market forever, but no one had snatched it up for re-development yet.

It seemed our killer had turned the former oasis into an island of horrors.

48

Daniels cruised the patrol boat in with the surf, plowing the aluminum bottom boat into the shallows. JD and I hopped into the water, trudged to the beach, and advanced to the tree line with our weapons in the firing position.

The island had slowly taken back the resort. Asphalt paths were cracked and overgrown with weeds and foliage. The tennis courts were faded and cracked. The pool looked like it was home to a creature from another dimension. The cabanas had been boarded up, but many of the boards had been ripped out. Siding had been torn off, and roofs had collapsed. Some buildings were nothing more than piles of rubble. Others had weathered the storms without much damage.

JD and I swept through the premises, clearing the area.

My heart pounded with anticipation. We cleared the rooms one by one. They were littered with debris—empty beer bottles, tattered clothing, used condoms, syringes. It was evident people had squatted in them over the years. Threw parties. Did God knows what.

They were built on stilts to avoid the rising water, but the resort was no match for the force of the hurricanes. The steps leading up to each room creaked and groaned, and some could barely hold weight.

We didn't find Reagan in any of the cabins on the west side of the island.

A sour acidic taste crept in the back of my throat as my stomach twisted. I feared we might never find her.

We crossed what used to be the main lobby, moving to the east side of the island. We passed dilapidated sand volleyball courts, shuffleboard, and the remains of an outdoor bar.

We reached another set of cabins and searched one by one.

A wave of relief washed over me when we found Reagan.

She was bound and gagged, laying atop an old, stained mattress. Tears had streaked her mascara, and her hair was ratty and disheveled. I knelt beside her and removed the gag from her mouth and untied her bonds.

She flung her arms around me and held tight.

"Are you okay?"

"Yeah," she said, sobbing.

"He didn't hurt you, did he?"

"No."

I didn't want to let go of her. I could feel her heart pounding against mine.

"How did you find me?" she asked.

I told her the story.

I helped Reagan to her feet. She was weak and dehydrated. I gave her a bottle of water when we got back to the sheriff's patrol boat. She guzzled it down in a matter of moments.

"I'm gonna look around the island," JD said. "See If I can find anyone else."

He disappeared back into the forest.

The island was small—half a mile across, and a mile long.

"What can you tell me about him?" I asked.

"Not much," Reagan said. "He wore a mask. I never saw his face. He was a big guy. 6'1", maybe 6'2". 200 pounds? I'm not real good with that kind of thing."

"Would you recognize his voice?"

"Maybe?"

After a cursory search of the island, JD returned. "There's nobody else here."

JD pushed us into the surf, and I helped him aboard. Sheriff Daniels cranked up the engines, and he angled the vessel back out to sea.

Reagan didn't want to go to the hospital. She just wanted to go home, take a shower, and get something to eat. "I need to wash this whole experience off me. Then I need a nice bottle of wine."

I chuckled, relieved to see her in good spirits. But I knew the psychological effects of a traumatic experience could manifest itself over the next several days, weeks, or months.

We bounced across the water, racing back to Coconut Key. Reagan curled beside me, my arm around her.

"Thanks for rescuing me," she said.

"Well, I figured I probably ought to. I mean the news just wasn't the same without you."

She smacked my chest playfully.

Back at the sheriff's office, Reagan filled out a police report, and JD and I filled out an after action report.

Afterward, JD drove Reagan home, and I followed on my bike. A swarm of reporters waited. As soon as Reagan stepped out of Jack's Porsche, the cameras closed in, and microphones were shoved in her face.

"What can you tell us about the killer?"

"Do you know his identity?"

"Can you tell us what he did to you?"

Reagan and I pushed through the horde, and I escorted her inside the house.

Jack got out of there as soon as he could. He said he would catch up with me later.

Reagan breathed a sigh of relief and leaned against the front door after she latched it. "I'm going to take a shower, grab a change of clothes, then you and I are checking into the *Seven Seas.* I don't think I can stay here. I just don't feel safe."

"That's probably a good idea."

"Please tell me you have some idea who this guy is?"

"I'm pretty sure I know. Proving it might be a different story though."

Reagan frowned. “Who?”

“Erik Cain. Nurse at the hospital.”

Her eyes widened, and rage boiled on her face. She didn’t have to say anything.

“Trust me, I’m working on it.”

Reagan moved into the bedroom, peeled off her clothes, and slipped into the bathroom. She twisted the shower knobs, and the water sprayed into the stall.

I checked the premises, making sure to look into the closets and underneath the beds this time. I made sure all the windows were locked and all the doors secured.

After her shower, Reagan got dressed, packed a bag, and she took her car over to the *Seven Seas.* I followed on my bike. We had to fight our way through the horde of reporters, and dozens of them followed us to the hotel. It was a crazy caravan of news vans.

The rude woman that wouldn't rent me a room was behind the desk. We checked in and got a 4th floor unit that overlooked the water. We pushed into the room, and Reagan fell onto the bed and exhaled.

I stowed her bag in the closet, then climbed onto the bed beside her. She rolled on her side and curled around me. I lay there, stroking her hair, appreciating the moment. "How are you doing?"

"Never better," she said.

She was putting on a good front, but an experience like she'd been through had to mess with a person.

"If you want to talk about it, we can. If you don't, we won't. I'm here. Whatever you need."

She smiled and kissed my cheek. "Thank you."

She rested her head against my shoulder.

We stayed like that for a few moments, then she said, "I need food. And wine. Possibly whiskey. Probably a lot."

49

I had a hunch, and I was right.

We had never recovered the heads, or the hands, of the victims. I figured this was partially to obscure their identity. But I knew most of these sick bastards liked to re-live the crime over and over again. They would often revisit crime scenes and dump-sites. The killer would want to keep souvenirs close by.

We brought cadaver dogs to *Crystal Key Island.* It didn't take long for the astute canines to indicate over a grave-sight. We unearthed several grisly remains and were later able to match them to known victims. The remains were in different states of composition. The most recent victim's head was still relatively intact.

Unearthing the burial site wasn't for the faint of heart.

Brenda collected the remains and brought them to the lab for analysis. We needed something to connect Erik Cain to the crimes. A strand of hair. A sample of DNA from skin or bodily fluids.

Brenda called me a few days later with repulsive news. "You know that DNA saliva swab we took from Erik when you guys brought him in for questioning? Well, we got a positive match with semen found on one of the victim's remains."

I was both ecstatic and disgusted by the news.

"It seems like he continued to defile the victims even after they were dismembered."

I tried not to visualize the gruesome act, but it was already too late. "Thanks, Brenda."

"Go get that son-of-a-bitch!"

“You got it.”

The evidence was enough to convince the DA to move forward. The judge issued a warrant for Erik Cain’s arrest, and Sheriff Daniels sent JD and I to collect the suspect.

I hopped into JD's Porsche and we raced to the hospital. I flashed my badge and displayed the warrant at the front desk, then pushed through the double doors into the patient area of the emergency room.

Erik Cain stood in the hallway, talking to Dr. Parker. The scumbag’s eyes widened as soon as he saw us. There was no smug grin on his face this time. By the determined look in my eyes, I'm sure he was able to tell we had something on him.

He turned and ran down the hallway.

I gave chase. "Freeze! We have a warrant for your arrest!"

My words did nothing.

Erik's footsteps echoed down the hallway as I chased after him.

JD wasn't far behind.

The suspect twisted and turned through the maze of hallways, weaving through nurses and patients. It was a dangerous proposition. Barreling into someone with a medical emergency wouldn't be good.

Erik slipped past two nurses wheeling a man in a hospital bed down the hallway. He grabbed the railing and rotated the bed, blocking the path.

The patient groaned, the railing rattled, and the bag of IV fluids swayed.

The bed obstructed the hallway and slowed me down enough to lose sight of Erik as he rounded the corner.

After a moment, the nurses cleared the hallway, and I resumed my sprint. When I rounded the corner, Erik was nowhere in sight.

There was a bathroom on the left, several patient rooms on the right, and an exit door at the end of the hallway.

With my weapon drawn, I edged forward.

JD took the restroom.

I peered into the rooms, then advanced toward the exit.

The blinding sun squinted my eyes as I pushed through the door into the parking lot. It took a second for my eyes to adjust. I scanned from left to right and caught sight of Erik slipping into a black Mustang.

He cranked up the engine, dropped the car into gear, and

spun the tires. Smoke wafted from the wheel wells as he screeched out of the lot.

JD burst through the door a moment later.

We ran to the Porsche which Jack had parked in the red zone at the curb near the entrance to the ER. I hopped in the passenger seat, and JD cranked up the flat six. He popped the clutch and peeled out of the parking lot.

We turned onto the highway, chasing after the black Mustang. Jack ran through the gears with precision, and a few moments later, we were hitting triple digits, racing down the blacktop.

The Mustang was fast!

But the 3.8 liter flat six was faster.

Erik weaved in and out of traffic, swerving around slower cars.

I could see him dart in and out in the distance.

JD had the pedal mashed to the floor.

110 MPH...

120 MPH...

130 MPH...

140 MPH...

The acceleration pinned me against the seat. The roar of the engine filled the cabin. With the top down, the wind swirled around, tossing my hair.

Jack jammed on the brakes as we caught up to the traffic.

The blacktop highway had two lanes moving in each direction, divided by a grassy esplanade.

JD carved through the traffic. The Porsche hugged the ground with hot, sticky rubber. As soon as we made it through the clump of slower cars, JD floored it again, and soon we were nearing 150 MPH.

The Mustang had to slow down at the next cluster of traffic, and we finally caught up to Erik.

I angled my weapon out the window as JD pulled up behind the black vehicle.

Erik wasn't going to stop.

There was no lawyering his way out of this one. We had him dead to rights.

Or so I thought.

Erik stuck a pistol out the driver's side window and aimed it back at us. Muzzle flash flickered from the barrel, and bullets streaked through the air.

He didn't even aim the damn thing. He couldn't. He was just hoping against hope he'd get lucky and hit something.

I was done playing games. I took aim at his back tire and squeezed off two rounds.

The tire burst with a loud pop, then shredded shortly thereafter. The highway tore it to pieces. Amber sparks showered from the rim as it carved into the blacktop.

The Mustang got squirrelly, and Jack hit the brakes.

Erik cranked the wheel and veered to the left, crossing over the highway, nearly missing the oncoming traffic.

Horns honked.

Cars jammed their brakes.

Tires squealed.

The engine roared as the Mustang barreled down an unpaved road into a gravel yard.

Jack jammed the brakes and we waited at the esplanade for the traffic to clear. A moment later, we crossed the highway and chased after the Mustang.

Erik left a trail of dust in the air. It made him easy to follow, but it brought visibility down.

I coughed as the dust hit my lungs.

Jack followed the Mustang into the gravel yard. Piles of sand and limestone towered above. There were heavy rock grinders used to crush and sort stone. There were plenty of trucks and heavy machinery. Large yellow backhoes, loaders, excavators. Rows and rows of dump trucks. Conveyers transported the sorted rock to various piles.

It reminded me of a vast desert with towering dunes.

We slowed as we entered the yard, the piles of gravel creating a giant maze.

Erik was in here somewhere.

50

We followed the trail of dust, gravel crunching underneath our tires. I kept my weapon at the ready as we snaked around the man-made dunes. We moved into a clearing where Erik had done several donuts, kicking up as much dust as possible. It hung in the air like a storm cloud.

He had done it to cover his tracks. There was no telling which pathway he had disappeared down.

We sat in the clearing for a moment, waiting for the dust to settle.

A backhoe operator pointed us in the right direction.

We followed the path as it curved around the dunes. I called the sheriff and informed him of the situation.

Backup was on the way.

We crept through a narrow canyon, like a predator stalking its prey. Dusty haze hung in the air.

The Mustang launched from a side road. The car barreled toward us and slammed into the driver's side door. The impact lifted us on two wheels and twisted the car around before we plopped down.

It was a good thing there were steel reinforced safety beams in the door, or JD would have been dead.

As it stood, he had a hell of a headache.

So did I.

The Mustang backed up, jammed the breaks, then Erik twisted the wheel and mashed the gas. The remaining rear tire spit gravel as he took off, heading back the way we came. Gravel flew through the air, pelting the Porsche.

Erik fired two shots at us as he departed.

The black car hobbled along with the rim grinding into the gravel road.

The Porsche had stalled out after the impact, and JD couldn't get it started. I hopped out of the car and chased after the Mustang.

The impact must have cracked the radiator because the ground was drenched with coolant. Steam billowed from underneath the Mustang's hood, but it kept chugging along.

Until an excavator operator swung the bucket into the side of the Mustang.

The heavy piece of machinery collapsed the passenger side door and shoveled the car across the gravel like it was a toy in a sandbox.

The engine gave up the ghost.

Erik tried desperately to restart the car. He twisted the key, and the starter warbled.

The engine never turned over. It had gone to the engine heaven in the sky.

Erik sprang from the car and took off on foot. He's sprinted across the clearing, and I watched him disappear down a pathway.

I chased after him and cautiously entered the valley of gravel. I advanced with my weapon in the firing position, weaving down the narrow trail.

Gunfire erupted as I reached the next clearing.

Muzzle flash flickered, and bullets impacted piles of gravel beside me. I dove for cover behind a mound as plumes of dust exploded.

I angled my weapon around the berm.

Erik had taken cover behind a giant rock crusher. He blasted several more shots in my direction. The gravel spidered with debris and chips of rocks.

The rock crusher was in the center of the clearing. There were two dump trucks to the left, and a yellow backhoe to the right that was empty.

There were no gravel yard workers in the area. I blasted several shots at Erik.

Bang!

Bang!

Pop!

Something was wrong.

The weapon had fouled.

I ducked for cover behind the berm and addressed the situation. I knew what had happened the moment I heard the *pop*. In all my years of handling a weapon, it only had happened once before when I was using re-loads.

But this was factory ammunition!

I dropped the magazine and racked the slide.

There was a bullet stuck in the barrel.

The load had been insufficient and lacked the power to propel the bullet out of the barrel. Had I ignored the *pop* and chambered another round, the results could have been disastrous.

The weapon was useless until I was able to clear the jam. And I'd need to disassemble the weapon to do that.

I peered around the berm, and more bullets peppered the gravel nearby.

I ducked for cover, waited a moment, holstered the weapon, then sprinted toward a dump truck.

The scumbag fired two more shots at me as I ran across the clearing.

Plumes of dust sprouted at my feet.

I took cover behind the giant right front tire of the dump truck. I inched back and grabbed the passenger door handle. The door was unlocked, and I swung it open. I crawled inside and crouched down in the passenger seat.

Erik fired two more shots, webbing the front windshield with cracks. Shards of glass sprayed about the cabin.

I climbed over the transmission into the driver seat.

More bullets peppered the glass.

I pulled the visor down and the keys dropped into my hand. I shoved them into the ignition and twisted.

The engine roared to life.

I ducked below the dash as Erik fired a few more shots, pinging against the door and putting another web of cracks into the windshield.

I put the truck in gear, let out the clutch, and rolled forward. I twisted the wheel, angling the vehicle around the far side of the crusher, then circled around toward Erik.

I kept low, peering over the dash.

Erik took off running down another pathway, and I chased him down in the behemoth.

I wanted to run the son-of-a-bitch over. It would be so satisfying to feel his skull collapse under the weight of the massive tires. I wanted to mow him over like a speedbump in a mall parking lot.

I usually wasn't prone to such vengeful thoughts, but this guy had pissed me off.

Erik angled the gun over his shoulder and fired several shots into the windshield and engine compartment of the dump truck.

After a few shots, the slide of his gun locked forward—the magazine was empty.

He didn't reload.

Out of magazines, he stuffed the weapon in his holster.

I hit the brakes and killed the engine. I hopped out of the cab and chased after the scumbag.

Erik was fast.

My legs drove me forward, and my chest heaved for breath. My quads burned as I sprinted as fast as I could.

I leapt into the air and tackled the cretin. We crashed to the dirt, and I climbed on top of him, pummeling him in the face—getting a little payback for the baseball bat I took to the head.

Erik bucked me off, and I rolled aside.

I sprang to my feet, and we squared off against each other like two heavyweight prize fighters. We circled each other, looking for a point of attack.

He charged and swung hard.

I blocked, punched him in the rib cage, then tried to twist his arm into an arm-bar takedown—but he wasn't having any of it.

He twisted around, broke free, then did a roundhouse kick.

Erik was well trained.

He knew how to fight and was combat tested.

I leaned back as his foot whiffed in front of my face.

I caught his leg, then planted a swift kick into his balls.

He groaned in agony.

With my elbow, I jammed down on the side of his knee.

Ligaments snapped.

Erik would never walk again without a limp.

He fell to the ground, then staggered to his feet, but I kicked him in the face before he could get up.

His jaw snapped shut, and teeth shattered.

Blood spewed from his lips.

He fell back against the dirt.

The patter of a news helicopter hovered overhead.

Distant sirens wailed.

Reinforcements would be here soon. I only had a few minutes to serve up a dish of cold revenge.

I wasn't going to kill the guy—just beat him within an inch of his life.

He staggered to his feet, blood trickling down his chin. He looked like a crazed maniac with a bloody face and wide eyes. It was a glimpse of his inner demon.

Then he did something I didn't anticipate.

He pulled a switch-blade from his back pocket and flipped it open with the press of a button. An evil grin curled on his gnarled face as he brandished the weapon.

This definitely brought a new dimension to the fight.

51

The first rule of knife fighting is *don't get into a knife fight.* It's a lose-lose proposition. One of you will probably die on site, and the other will probably die on the way to the hospital. There are too many variables to contend with, and no margin for error.

When a guy starts aggressively swinging a blade, all bets are off.

Defensive cuts on the wrists and forearms can render you incapacitated rather quickly. A sharp blade can cut through tendons and nerves with ease. You won't be able to make a fist, and you'll bleed out quicker than you think.

I'd take a short range gunfight over a knife fight any day. Fine motor skills degrade with nerves and the rush of adrenaline. Roughly 80% of shots fired miss their targets. It's a high stress environment, and most people don't get an accurate *sight picture.* They just point and shoot and hope for the best.

Erik charged at me, the blade glimmering in the sunlight.

I moved back as he advanced.

He slashed across the body twice.

I managed to avoid both.

The blade carved through the air with a swoosh. Then Erik stabbed at my torso as he charged again.

I grabbed his forearm and pinned his wrist against my left hip, the tip of the blade precariously close to my skin. I kneed him in the balls twice.

He groaned and doubled over, and I finished with an elbow to the bridge of his nose.

Blood splattered, and he staggered back.

I kept his arm pinned, and chopped down on his elbow.

The knife fell from his hand and bounced against the dirt.

Erik came back with a hard left hook. His knuckles smacked my cheek, wrenching my head to the side. It felt like a brick had smacked me in the head.

The boy packed a punch.

He broke free of my grasp and kicked me in the belly. It doubled me over, and I dropped to my knees, the wind knocked out of me.

Then he kicked me in the face.

Talk about a chiropractic adjustment!

My head snapped back, and blood spewed from my lips. The blow twisted me around, sending me crashing to the dirt. Blood dotted the ground.

The world spun.

My vision blurred.

It took me a second to regroup.

I heard his heavy footsteps crunch against the gravel behind me, and a long shadow fell over me.

The blade glimmered in the sunlight nearby, shining like a brilliant star.

My hand snatched the knife, and I spun around, just as Erik pounced on top of me.

I jammed the knife into his belly with several quick stabs. With the final puncture, I carved an L shape into his gut, pulling the knife up to the rib cage. It was a lethal move.

I pulled my blood soaked hand away.

Erik wouldn't recover from the wound.

His eyes went wide, and he dropped to his knees momentarily, clutching his bloody belly. There was no stemming the tide.

He finally fell face down in the dirt.

A river of crimson blood stained the beige gravel.

The news helicopter caught the whole thing on video. It would be replayed endlessly on the evening news and on the Internet.

Erik rolled onto his back and gurgled for breath as his lungs filled with fluid. A volcano of blood spewed from his mouth when he coughed. It speckled his face and drizzled onto the sand. His chest heaved, and a last breath rattled from his lungs.

His body went still.

I wondered how many innocent victims had suffered the tip of that blade? How many had he killed that we didn't know about?

Standing over his lifeless body, I had a twinge of regret. He got off way too easy. Then I reminded myself of the utter torment and torture that awaited him in the afterlife. I had been to hell before, and I never wanted to go back. Erik would become a permanent resident.

I knelt beside the corpse and put the pads of my fingers on his neck, feeling for a pulse.

He was most certainly dead.

The helicopter pattered overhead, circling the area.

Several patrol cars raced into the gravel yard, red and blue lights flashing. They pulled to the scene and jammed the brakes. Gravel crunched under their tires as they skidded to a halt, kicking up plumes of dust.

Sheriff Daniels hopped out of his patrol car, and JD staggered around a dune.

We gathered not far from the body.

"Karma's a bitch, ain't it?" JD said, amused by the bloody corpse.

Daniels surveyed the grim scene. He looked mildly pleased. He gave me a nod of approval, then he looked up at the news helicopter. “They’re going to have a field day with this.”

“You’re a shoo-in for re-election now,” I said. “*The man who’s department saved Coconut Key!*”

“We’ll see,” he muttered.

“We need to talk about reimbursement for property damage during the pursuit," JD said with a hopeful smile.

Daniels gave him a stone face.

Jack's smile faded. "My Porsche is trashed!”

Daniels remained expressionless.

“Just think of all the money we saved the taxpayers, avoiding a long trial, multiple appeals, a stay on death row?"

After a long moment, Daniels relented. "Submit an expense report with receipts.”

Jack smiled. "Thanks, boss."

We waited for the medical examiner and the forensics team to arrive. Before long, the scene was swarmed with LEOs and EMTs.

I got a bottle of water and cleansing scrub from an EMT and washed the blood from my hands.

News vans flooded into the gravel yard, surrounding the perimeter of the crime scene. The deputies struggled to contain them.

Reagan wasn't among them.

Reporters shouted questions. "Can you confirm that is, in fact, the *Sandcastle Killer?*"

"Was the use of deadly force absolutely necessary?"

"How did you link him to the crimes?"

I ignored them.

Jack called a tow truck for the Porsche. After it was loaded onto the flatbed, we rode with a deputy back to the station. There was lots of paperwork, and I went through all the usual protocols when an officer kills a suspect in the line of duty.

I'm sure there would be plenty of debate. I stabbed an unarmed man. No doubt, in this day and age, someone would take Erik's side.

I was put on administrative leave as a matter of routine.

I could use the time off.

As we wrapped up at the sheriff's office, JD was still grumbling about his Porsche. "Man, I loved that car."

"So, get it fixed."

He shook his head. "It will never be the same. Do you know how hard it is to match custom paint? Plus, if the frame is bent, it will chew through tires. They'll never get the alignment right."

I think he was just making excuses in order to justify a new car.

He rubbed his neck and groaned, still sore from the impact.

"Did you get checked out by the EMTs?" I asked.

He looked at me like I was crazy.

"You might want to get looked at," I said. "Rule out any soft tissue injuries."

"Nothing a shot of whiskey and an ice pack can't fix."

"Just don't start in on the pain meds again."

His eyes narrowed at me. "Yes, dear."

We shared a cab back to his place, then the driver took me to Reagan's.

She pulled open the door, and I stepped into the foyer. She greeted me with a warm hug and a long embrace.

I could get used to this sort of thing.

"I watched the footage on the news," she said.

"I'm a little surprised I didn't see you there?"

"I figured I'd get the story straight from the horse's mouth sooner or later." She smiled. "Besides, I said I wasn't giving that guy anymore publicity."

"Well, he's not going to hurt anybody anymore," I said.

"He could have hurt you," she said in a worried tone.

I dismissed it as nonsense.

"I'm glad you're safe," she cooed.

"Careful, I might start to think you care," I said.

"I do," she whispered.

She lifted on her tiptoes and planted her full lips against

mine. She expressed her gratitude in the most sublime of ways.

Over the next few days, I decompressed at Reagan's house. She took time off from the station, and we spent most of our time trying to wear out her mattress.

I think we made a pretty good effort.

We were occasionally hounded by reporters, looking for an interview. I wasn't about to open my mouth and say anything until the internal investigation had been resolved.

A few days later, I got a call from the *Coconut Key Animal Shelter.* Someone had found Fluffy and brought her to the shelter. I had updated the owner information on her collar. It seemed that whoever had stolen the *Wild Tide* was decent enough to let the animal out on dry land.

I borrowed Reagan's car and cruised down to the shelter and picked up the snobby cat. She looked indifferent about seeing me again. But that was par for the course for a cat.

I took Fluffy over to *Diver Down.* Madison had been looking after Buddy for me, and now he had his companion back.

Buddy bounced up and down and barked, wagging his tail when he saw me. I knelt down and petted the little guy and gave him a big hug. I leashed him up, and we went for a short walk.

The afternoon was gorgeous, it was good to spend time with Buddy. I liked staying with Reagan, but I missed being on the water. Being able to step out of the salon and be in the open air. Feel the breeze and watch the sunrise over the water with a cup of coffee. Every day in the Keys reminded me of a painting by a master artist. The island paradise was living art.

I brought Buddy back to Madison, then drove back to Reagan's. She was in the kitchen, uncorking a bottle of red wine. She poured two glasses and had a little smile on her face. "We're celebrating. Sort of."

I looked at her, curiously. "What are we celebrating?"

"I got an amazing job offer!"

My brow lifted, surprised. "That's fantastic!"

"And, I got a book deal."

"Really?"

"*48 Hours with a Killer,*" she said. "A true crime memoir."

"Congratulations!"

We clinked glasses and sipped the Merlot.

“I thought you weren’t giving the killer any more publicity?"

“Well, he's dead, and the publisher offered me a seven-figure advance."

"Nothing like money to compromise one's integrity," I said, teasing her.

Her eyes narrowed at me.

She was silent for a long moment.

"There's one small issue," Reagan added.

I gave her a look, encouraging her to continue.

"The job is with a national news network. This could be a huge opportunity for my career."

I knew there were no national news stations based in Coconut Key. "Where is the job at?"

"I'd have to move to Los Angeles if I took the job." She cringed, anticipating my response.

My heart sank. The oxygen left my lungs. My stomach knotted.

I took a breath and put on a good face. I didn't really want to see her go. But I wasn't going to hold her back from pursuing her dreams. "If it's a good opportunity, I think you should take it."

She looked conflicted. "Really?"

"Yes, really," I said. "How often do opportunities like this come along? This is something you've wanted your whole career. You can't just blow it off."

"What does that mean for us?"

I shrugged. "I guess we'll have to wait and see."

Her big beautiful eyes looked up at me. "You're not mad, are you?"

"Why would I be mad?"

She moved close. "I'm definitely going to miss you. You can come visit?" She lifted up and kissed me. "I'm definitely going to miss those lips."

"There are a few things about you I'll miss as well," I said, with a sly grin.

"Oh yeah, like what?"

"Well, you're kind... You're loving... And..."

"And?" she asked, fishing for more compliments.

"You've got a great ass."

"And?" she asked with a grin, still wanting more.

"I don't think there's anything about you I won't miss," I said.

"Good answer."

She gave me another passionate kiss. Then she took my hand and pulled me into the bedroom, determined to give me a taste of everything that I would be missing.

Incentive for me to come visit.

A *lot* of incentive.

52

When the day finally came for Reagan to leave—and the movers had loaded the last box onto the truck—there were hugs, tears, kisses, and heartfelt promises.

We said our last goodbyes, and I soaked in her gorgeous face with my eyes. I tasted her lips one last time, then watched her hop into her car and drive away.

When she left, she took a piece of me.

I climbed on my bike and rode back to *Diver Down* and took a seat at the bar, looking deflated. I needed some aqua therapy. There was nothing like getting out on the water to forget about all my troubles.

The only problem—I didn't have a boat.

I needed to remedy that situation.

I called JD after I ordered a burger. "I'm officially homeless. Reagan just left."

"And how does that make you feel?" JD asked, almost mocking me.

"I don't need a therapy session, I need a place to live."

"There's always my couch."

"That's not a long-term solution."

"Well, I've been thinking about this. Since you've got a little cash now, and it looks like insurance is going to pay out a decent amount, I thought we might go in on something together? Pool our resources, get twice as much?"

I thought about it for a moment. "I don't know. That's kind of like getting married. You know how I feel about commitment."

"Relax. You've got more than enough Hollywood money to buy me out if you think I nag too much."

I rolled my eyes.

"Besides. We could move up to a higher level of clientele. I'm thinking we go for supreme luxury. A party boat for the rich and famous. Plus, I think this photography thing might take off. I got a call from a bikini company that wants to do a shoot. So, we need to find something, ASAP!"

"What are you doing tomorrow?" I asked.

"You and I are going looking for a new boat," Jack said.

"Alright. That sounds like a deal. Did you get the Porsche back yet?"

"Hell no. They are waiting on a part from Germany. I'm looking at six weeks. Some proprietary motor for the door window. I'm thinking about selling it and getting another one. There's a guy in the body shop that made an offer. It's a little low, but I'm considering it. I might be able to squeeze a few extra dollars out of him." He paused. "They gave me a loaner, so I'll pick you up in the morning. Where are you staying tonight?"

"I don't know. I might crash on Madison's couch. I might go over to the *Seven Seas."*

"Okay. Just let me know."

There was a moment of silence.

"How are you holding up?" JD asked.

"I'm fine. Why wouldn't I be fine?"

"I don't know. Seems like you kinda liked that girl."

"I'm totally fine. I promise. I'll see you tomorrow." I hung up the phone as my eyes misted.

I pretended I had a lash in my eye and wiped the wetness away. I clenched my jaw, fighting back the lump in my throat. I had remained cool, but it finally hit me that Reagan was gone.

My phone rang again.

This time it was Isabella. "You know the gentleman you asked me to find? Esteban Rivera? I don't have an exact location, but I do have an asset that saw him six weeks ago."

My eyes perked up. "Where?"

Ready for more?

Join my newsletter and find out what happens next!

AUTHOR'S NOTE

Thanks for all the great reviews!

I'm curious to know if anyone tried to solve the ciphers? I had fun making the notes and drawing the suspect sketch. Let me know if you want more of that stuff.

I've got more adventures for Tyson and JD. Stay tuned.

If you liked this book, let me know with a review on Amazon.

Thanks for reading!

—*Tripp*

TYSON WILD

Wild Ocean

Wild Justice

Wild Rivera

Wild Tide

Wild Rain

Wild Captive

Wild Killer

Wild...

MAX MARS

The Orion Conspiracy

Blade of Vengeance

The Zero Code

Edge of the Abyss

Siege on Star Cruise 239

Phantom Corps

The Auriga Incident

Devastator

CONNECT WITH ME

I'm just a geek who loves to write. Follow me on Facebook.

TRIPP ELLIS

www.trippellis.com

Made in United States
North Haven, CT
21 March 2023